# BORN SAVAGE

Ordway was bringing in the two thousand head of cattle that would make his ranch the biggest in the area. After the long trail drive he just wanted to settle down and marry his pretty fiancée. But things had changed since he'd left. On his way to town he found his friends leveling their guns at him and his girl had already married his worst enemy. But Ordway was born savage and he swore he'd kill every man in town unless he found out what the hell had happened. His homecoming was the spark that would touch off the biggest range war the territory had ever seen.

# BORN SAVAGE

## William Hopson

ATLANTIC LARGE PRINT
Chivers Press, Bath, England.
John Curley & Associates Inc.,
South Yarmouth, Mass., USA.

MAY 7 1984

**Library of Congress Cataloging in Publication Data**

Hopson, William.
  Born savage.

  "Atlantic large print."
  1. Large type books.   I. Title.
PS3515.06526B6   1984      813'.54      83–15317
ISBN 0–89340–639–2

---

**British Library Cataloguing in Publication Data**

Hopson, William
  Born savage.—Large print ed.—(Atlantic large print)
  I. Title
  813'.52[F]         PS3515.0/

  ISBN 0–85119–631–4

This Large Print edition is published by Chivers Press, England, and John Curley & Associates, Inc, U.S.A. 1984

Published by arrangement with Singer Communications Inc

U.K. Hardback ISBN  0  85119  631  4
U.S.A. Softback ISBN  0  89340  639  2

Photoset, printed and bound in Great Britain by
REDWOOD BURN LIMITED, Trowbridge, Wiltshire

# BORN SAVAGE

# CHAPTER ONE

Two thousand head of Mexican cattle, plus a few strays picked up on the long drive north to Colorado, lay soundless out there in the darkness when Channon Ordway awoke. The very stillness itself was what brought Ordway awake, all senses instantly alert. He was bedded down about seventy-five yards from where his crew of tired *vaqueros* had camped the evening before.

Ordway came up on an elbow, his .44 Colt six-shooter in a palm where it had lain all night. His damp slicker rustled loudly as he threw aside the blankets. The feeling that something was definitely wrong, again, clung clammily like the wet mist on his slicker.

He peered through the darkness and could see nothing.

Not a sound disturbed his ears. No night riders in pairs circling the bedded down herd and singing softly the eternal love songs of Old Mexico. Ordway's tough grulla night horse, tethered a few feet away, stood dozing.

A horse sleeps soundest from two until

five, and Ordway knew from the slumped, hip-shot posture, plus a glance at the stars, that it must be about two hours before dawn.

Ordway rose like a dark cat and strapped on his gunbelt. Standing first on one wool-socked foot and then the other, he jerked on a pair of Mexican made boots weighted with ornate silver spurs. The rowels were made from drilled pesos, round and tineless. He had slept in half-length *chaparajas* of heavy thorn-proof leather.

When he added a huge red sombrero and slung a bandoleer of .45–70–500 cartridges over his left shoulder he looked to be exactly what he was: a tough, fighting man; survivor of a bloody but abortive revolution.

In this last respect he'd fared better than most of the others. He'd not only escaped with his life, he'd also brought out two thousand head of prime cattle to bring home to the Ordway ranch in Pronghorn Basin.

Within two minutes the blanket-slicker roll was cantle tied and Channon Ordway was ready. Carrying the short, ugly-looking carbine in his left hand, he crept warily through the menacing silence toward where the two-wheel, ox-drawn *carreta* containing their food and other trail supplies had been left the evening before.

All he found, however, were the ash-covered remains of the cook's banked fire.

The cook and crew, the cart; everybody and everything—had vanished as Ordway lay in slumber.

Ordinarily he would have heard them go. But there had been little sleep or rest for him since the day three weeks ago when Sonny Shackleford and Red Waldo and their cutthroat crew had made an attempted foray against the herd. Armed only with short-range repeaters, Sonny and Red had forgotten what oversized 500-grain slugs could do in the hands of a man who'd already killed Waldo's brother over a card table in Cheyenne.

In the face of such shocking power the notorious outfit had pulled off and disappeared to lick their wounds, the pudgy Waldo mounted behind one of the others.

And that was what puzzled Ordway now. His *vaqueros* had feared nothing in the universe short of God, the Devil, and their village priests. They'd fought beside Ordway in mounted battles. Yet they had

3

deserted like flimsy shadows.

'They probably rolled that oxcart back at least a half mile by hand before hooking on and lighting out,' Ordway told himself, a little in disbelief.

But why had they left without pay? And without the bonus?

His old Ute godfather had once said: *When you seek an enemy, think back, never ahead.* Ordway thought back. A name flashed into his mind.

'Why, of course,' he almost snorted at himself. 'Step Eaton!'

Ordway had been raised with Step as well as Sonny Shackleford in Tulac. It was Step who had accompanied him to Mexico as friend and guard over fifteen thousand dollars borrowed from Mike Adkins' bank in Tulac. They were to buy and drive back a herd of feeders to the Pronghorn spread, owned jointly by Channon and his gaunt uncle, Ethan.

But Step's greed apparently had got the best of him. He'd shot Channon Ordway in the back down there in Mexico, robbed him of the money, and left him to die in the Chihuahua desert. Ordway often had wondered if Step would have the nerve to come back home.

4

It now appeared a good guess that he had. He'd returned and pulled the wool over Ethan's eyes—and perhaps the blue ones of Kathy Perry. Maybe he'd thrown in with Sonny . . .

Ordway bent over a pile of brush, gathered by the cook the day before, and quickly built a fire over the coals. As it crackled into light he turned to get into the protection of the shadows. But he froze in sheer astonishment at the sight of a man who had materialized as mysteriously as the trail crew had disappeared.

The man stood back of a levelled sporting-type bird gun.

'That's right, old fellow,' he said pleasantly. 'Don't move!'

He came a step closer. 'Because if you do my very capable niece on the other side will shoot off an arm should I fail to do so.'

He was a fairly tall man in brown corduroy jodhpurs, dove-colored corduroy coat, with a cap of similar material and color. The odd thing about the cap was that in addition to a visor in front, it had a second visor slanting down at the back.

He was so obviously out of place in this wilderness country that under different circumstances Channon Ordway might

5

have silently considered him completely ridiculous.

But there was something about the man, the way he held the gun; something in the icy blue eyes that bespoke the hunter. This man was as deadly as a Mexican jungle jaguar.

Behind Ordway came another sound, the faint scuff of a soft, flat-heel leather boot. He twisted for a look. A girl in fringed leather riding skirt and purple blouse stepped into view. She too carried a light sporting-type shotgun with fancy engraving on the barrels and an ornately checkered stock.

Ordway hadn't seen that gun in fifteen years, since he'd been a boy of twelve.

He spoke equably to the cool man in jodhpurs. 'You're lucky the fire was crackling. Otherwise I'd have dropped you in your tracks.'

'Would you now?' the voice was spiced with dry toleration. 'I've hunted wild animals in many places, my friend. So has my niece.'

Ordway studied her closely. She was bareheaded with copper-colored tresses in a tight bun at the back of her neck. But it was her eyes that startled him. He would have

6

sworn they held a faint obsidian cast. Black as his own and yet different. They shone with a strange luster.

He spoke to her uncle. 'We're wasting time and I've got a herd on my hands. Who are you and what do you want?'

The man, equally strange in his own way, gave a reproving chuckle. 'You disappoint me, Mr. Ordway. I've been told I bear a strong resemblance to an eccentric older brother who bought Squaw Valley a few miles below Pronghorn Basin and lived there in solitude.'

'Wentworth Randolph? The Hermit?'

'Of course. You shot him to death the day you left for Mexico in order to have his land when you returned with cattle.'

'Is that a fact?' Ordway snorted disgustedly.

'Quite. Unfortunately for you and your terrible uncle, you over-looked the possibility of heirs. I'm Eric Randolph and Mrs. Randolph is at the ranch. This is my niece, Vernell.'

'Pleased to meet you, I'm sure,' the girl responded correctly, and with the proper amount of hostility to match.

'Are you now?' Channon Ordway suddenly grinned at her. He shoot that

7

crazy Hermit? Old Sheriff Tobe Whitehouse, who had been one of the old outlaw bunch, and his deputy Bob Koonce, another of the outlaw kids like Ordway and Sonny and Step Eaton—they'd straighten out this idiotic mess in a hurry!

The girl sensed the snorting contempt going through the wild-looking, black-whiskered man from Mexico. Her half-raised weapon went all the way to her shoulder. The small double bores shifted until they were aimed at Ordway's right arm.

'Drop your rifle first, Mr. Ordway,' she directed quietly. 'And please let it fall easily. Every man has one weakness and Eric's compelling one is good guns. He undoubtedly plans to add yours to his collection after you pay the penalty for the murder of Wentworth Randolph.'

Ordway dutifully eased the Sharps single-shot to the grass beside his spurred boots. He stared blandly at a brief expanse of her legs between the hem of the riding skirt and the tops of her boots. She knew it was deliberate, that he was baiting her, and he grinned when the desired flush of anger came to her cheeks.

She was a far cry from little Kathy

Perry's wholesome prettiness, but ...
*Santa Maria*, how she could make a man's
pulse pound!

'All right. Now what's next?' he
enquired interestedly of her.

'Watch him, Eric, while I secure his
revolver,' she said to her uncle. 'It seems
incredible, but Step Eaton has warned us
that he can draw it from the sheath and fire
it in less than one second.'

Well, Ordway thought, all doubt now
gone. So Step *had* returned home with that
stolen money after all. Just couldn't give up
the idea of getting Kathy, huh?

So now there'd be a gun job to do in
Tulac once Ordway finished fooling around
with this loco greenhorn and his tiger cat
niece.

He made no move as the girl stepped in
from behind, leaned forward, and with
outstretched hand gingerly plucked the .44
Colt from its worn sheath.

Ordway spoke over his shoulder. 'An old
Ute Indian who was around when I was
born always said to be curious about your
enemies.'

'Indeed,' she sniffed, circling away as
though to get upwind from something that
had been dead for a few days.

9

'How did you get rid of my tail crew? How and why?'

The sardonic amusement in his black eyes was too much for her. He was supposed to curse, to argue, to deny. He should have clenched his fists in helpless anger and roared at them—anything except look at her with hidden laughter dancing wickedly in his own black eyes.

She was the one who lost control. 'Tell the murderer, Uncle Eric!' she cried out passionately. 'Tell him why we are taking his cattle!'

'Yes, you do that, Uncle Eric,' Channon Ordway chided, 'before she busts a corset.'

'It's quite simple, Mr. Ordway. When we arrived here to take over Squaw Valley, we found Ethan Ordway already in possession. When the two of you planned and executed old Went, you apparently didn't count upon the possibility of legal heirs.'

'Naturally not,' Ordway nodded agreeably. 'I expect that Ethan was plumb flabbergasted.'

'Not at all. In fact, it took a court order from Denver to dispossess him.'

'That doesn't account for you stealing my herd.'

Eric Randolph acted as though he hadn't heard. He went on: 'Once here, we saw tremendous possibilities and decided to remain and ranch, by stocking the valley with two thousand head of prime cattle.'

'Good idea,' Ordway approved. 'Only trouble is that only amateurs would try to stock at one whack. The neighbors might talk. What you shoulda done,' he chuckled, 'was wait until I got this herd home and then stole 'em from me a few head at a time.'

Eric Randolph's imperturbability faded. His voice turned grim.

'Yes, so we learned. That was exactly the way Ethan Ordway denuded Squaw Valley of every head of the two thousand stockers we bought and put on our newly inherited ranch.'

All the levity went out of Channon Ordway's eyes above the short black mustache and three weeks growth of whiskers. Every word this man spoke was probably true. Ethan Ordway had led Channon's own father into outlawry, which had cost his father his life. Ethan was a harsh, terrible man.

Like so many of the others who had reformed, Ethan was still, always had been,

11

an unregenerated outlaw at heart.

'What's the matter, Mr. Ordway?' the girl asked bitingly and with malicious relish. 'Do you find matters less amusing?'

'You misguided idiots!' he snapped at them. 'Give me time enough and I'll find out who took your cattle and where. And if Ethan Ordway is responsible settlement will be made. Tobe Whitehouse will see to that.'

The reply shocked him still more. 'Sheriff Whitehouse is dead these many months, my misguided friend. He was found murdered. Step Eaton is serving out the old fellow's unfinished term of office.'

'Step! Carrying old Tobe's badge?' Ordway was almost aghast.

'Except for his overindulgence at times, I assure you he'll see you hang.'

'Hang hell,' Ordway growled. 'Once he gets his handcuffs on me, I'll never live long enough to stand trial.'

The girl said, 'Shouldn't I have the men get the herd moving, Eric?'

'By all means, my dear. Tell Sonny Shackleford the prisoner has been disarmed and for him and Red Waldo to get the cattle under way at once while you and I take Mr. Ordway on ahead to the ranch.'

'Hold on!' Channon Ordway commanded.

'Yes?' It was the girl's turn to be amused and she made the most of it with a half smile of tolerance. She and her uncle had shaken this tough gun-fighter—shaken him hard.

'How come you're mixed up with that outfit?'

'An undesirable but undeniable necessity. As I understood it, you killed one of his men. In retaliation, he tried to raid your cattle three weeks ago, and,' the man gave a trace of a smile, 'has been licking his wounds and pride ever since. I offered him a generous percentage to let me plan the strategy. This time it seems to have been somewhat more successful.'

'Did Sonny ever tell you—didn't you ever hear that we were kids together in Tulac?' demanded Ordway incredulously.

'It's never been a habit of mine to listen to local gossip.'

'Neither did the Hermit,' snapped Ordway. 'It's one reason he probably was killed.'

The girl disappeared, mounted and rode away to where, no doubt, Sonny waited with his usual sneering grin. The slow

13

anger in Ordway rose steadily into a bright hot flame. If this aloof bird in his fancy britches had deigned to lower himself enough to make some friends, he'd have damn well avoided Sonny Shackleford and Red Waldo like the plague.

Presently the sound of several horses approached and grew loud. Randolph looked off among the trees and frowned.

'I ordered Sonny—' he began frigidly in the manner of a man accustomed to dealing with natives.

'Nobody orders Sonny Shackleford to do anything,' Ordway snapped, almost adding, 'except my uncle Ethan.'

He added furiously, 'Didn't anybody ever tell you that his old man was lynched as a desperado when Sonny was fourteen? Haven't you ever heard that he was an outlaw at fifteen, that he's been a leader of range hoodlums in Wyoming for the past several years?'

'Really, old fellow, you're beginning to annoy me immensely,' Eric Randolph said in the very best British ranch owner tradition.

Sounds of several people dismounting close beyond the firelight came loud and clear. The girl was the first to enter, her

14

face flushed with anger.

She said, 'They disobeyed you, Eric. Is it possible that in hiring this group of range ruffians you've allowed the camel to stick its head inside our tent?'

'I ain't no camel,' laughed Sonny Shackleford. 'I just wanted to see old Chann again after thinking he was dead all this time.'

Eric Randolph said icily, 'I'm not accustomed to having my orders disobeyed, Shackleford. Say what you wish and then get those cattle on their feet and moving. If Ethan Ordway knew about them ahead of their arrival, anything could happen.'

You poor, misguided damned fool, Ordway thought bitingly, and yet with a touch of pity. Hasn't anybody told you that Ethan has dominated Step and Sonny since they were kids in Tulac in the old outlaw days? Can't you get it through your head that this isn't Scotland or Vermont?

Sonny strode forward past the fire followed by his men. He was twenty-three now. Tawny, muscle-lithe, proud of his gun toughness. Sneering and arrogant because he dominated older men of his gang and even his pardner Red Waldo at times. Boastful that his father hadn't

15

waited to be hanged: he'd kicked the barrel from beneath his own feet.

A laugh broke from him and his yellow eyes danced wickedly as he looked at Ordway's *vaquero* clothing. The two men hadn't talked together since Channon had shot one of Sonny's men to death over a Cheyenne card table eighteen months before.

'Well, well!' Sonny jeered. 'So you got back home, huh, Chann? Shucks, ol' Step said you got killed in a revolution down in Mexico. Said you'd gone plumb native with half the gals down there before you got hit.'

He laughed again with a wicked glance at Vernell Randolph. Red Waldo, forty and heavy but packing little fat, edged in closer with a hard scowl. His red-rimmed eyes were unblinking.

'What else did Step say?' Ordway queried quietly. Best to find out what he could now. Both Sonny and his pardner Waldo had sworn to kill Ordway after that shoot-out in the Cheyenne saloon.

'He told Kathy she was a real beauty but that you musta thought them Mex gals much purtier. Said you had never intended to come back.'

Ordway turned and looked at Eric

Randolph as the men, at a covert signal from Red Waldo, began to converge.

'Mister, under other circumstances I could feel a little sorry for you but I don't. Anything you get from them you'll deserve. And that goes for you too, Miss.'

There was no time for reply because at that moment rough hands grabbed Channon Ordway from behind and pinioned his arms, and Red Waldo lunged forward and struck without further warning. His big fist smashed into Ordway's face.

Ordway acted instinctively. Even though he couldn't get his hands up for protection, he had instinctively rolled his head to one side and down. The brutish blow, struck at his mouth, hit crunchingly against the cheek bone beneath Ordway's left eye. His whole face went numb as he took the second blow in his mouth, and blood spurted.

The girl cried out. Randolph issued a crisp order in the voice of a man used to being obeyed. Sonny Shackleford laughed loudly.

Ordway, instead of straining at the hands holding him, suddenly lunged his full weight backward. It gave him room to lift a

17

Mexican boot and big spur holding a peso rowel of pure silver. The boot lashed out and caught Waldo squarely in the solar plexus.

A strangled 'ooof' went out of the short man as he half collapsed and clamped both hands to his stomach. He half bent at the waist, gasping for breath, and Sonny went off into howls of laughter at the expression on the stricken man's countenance.

Waldo straightened and sucked in a single long breath. There was murder in his eyes as he lunged again.

'Stop it!' the girl cried out, and Eric Randolph added his own voice to the din. But Sonny was enjoying himself too much and Waldo was insane with rage. He smashed blow after blow into Ordway's face.

'Now, damn you,' he panted fiercely. 'Here's where you pay fer killin' my brother!'

Pain was beginning to sicken Channon Ordway as he spat blood into the hated man's face. In his wildest imaginings he had never believed that anything like this could happen to him. Killed by a gun, yes. But not this.

Apparently the girl thought so too for she

herself put an end to it. Her light shotgun went to her shoulder, barrels elevated to the night sky and both hammers clicked. 'One more second, Mr. Shackleford, and I'll fire a shot that will stampede this herd back south for miles!'

'Hold it, boys,' Sonny laughed. 'That'll do, Reddie. You'll get more fun watching him stretch rope.'

Waldo stepped back as Ordway, his mustache blood-wet, spat again. Eric Randolph's eyes were sheer blue ice as he faced the young gang-leader. 'There seems to be a difference of opinion as to who gives the orders here, my friend. We're going to settle that right now.'

'Aw, now, wait a minute, Eric,' chuckled the young tough. 'I was raised with this catamount. He's tougher than his paw ever was.'

'And damn near as mean as Ethan,' panted Waldo, placing a finger against one side of his bulbous nose and blowing hard. 'You'll find out soon enough if he gits loose, Eric. Who's got some piggin' string?'

'I have,' Vernell Randolph said, surprisingly, and withdrew some from a pocket of her fringed riding skirt. 'I brought it along for this purpose.'

She looked straight at Ordway, still in the grip of four men. 'But please accept my word we had no intention of allowing matters to get out of hand.'

'That's a comfort,' he said dryly and spat wet red.

Maybe she felt justified, under circumstances, in picking out a man's role for herself in this conflict of hate and violence. Randolph's remarks about having night-hunted in far places, plus the deft, sure manner in which the girl handled a weapon explained much. But Ordway had been privately educated by a gentle eastern-bred mother who believed different, and had taught him the same ideals.

Like the brutal beating he'd received, he hadn't believed that such a thing as a woman handling a gun could happen, either.

Red Waldo drew the thongs viciously tight around Ordway's wrists, from behind, deliberately doing so to affect circulation. He stepped back with a grunt of satisfaction. 'There, that'll hold him for you two dudes.'

'Are you suggesting,' she said with asperity, 'that we are incapable of getting him safely into the hands of Sheriff Eaton?'

'I ain't suggestin' nothin', lady,' growled Waldo. 'All I know is he's Black Channon Ordway, he's killed seven men includin' my brother, and that if he gits loose he'll sure as hell kill yer four-eyed uncle.'

He said to Eric Randolph, 'If you got any sense you'll still ride outa here with that woman an' let us whip his hoss out from under a tree limb.'

'You have your orders,' snapped Randolph. 'Now get moving or I'll deal with you now.'

'How?' demanded Waldo, suddenly belligerent.

'Sonny,' Eric Randolph spoke to the younger leader. 'We are going to settle the matter of authority once and for all time, understand?'

'It's all settled boss,' Sonny replied almost meekly. 'What you say goes.'

Like hell Channon Ordway thought.

Ethan Ordway was mixed up in this. He had to be!

Ordway's giant, gaunt-faced, brooding uncle had wanted Squaw Valley ever since an eastern 'dude' had slipped in unobtrusively and bought it all. Now he intended to have it, and a hell of a lot more!

# CHAPTER TWO

Ordway's grulla night horse was led up. Rough hands boosted him into the saddle. Eric Randolph neck-tied the reins and then mounted his own horse with the grulla's tether rope in one hand.

The girl also was up and waiting, her light shotgun in a pommel sling. Her horse skittered sideways and before she could rein up she was almost beside Ordway, her eyes compellingly locking with his for one brief, hostile moment.

Whatever she saw in them—contempt, sardonic disdain—it brought a night-hidden flush to her cheeks. 'Well?' she challenged him. 'Say it, Mr. Ordway.'

'I once played poker with a hangman who'd executed twenty-seven criminals, Miss Randolph. First time, he said, made him a little sick. Along about the fifth he didn't mind. By the time he'd hung fifteen he was always real hungry afterward and ate a big plank steak.'

'What in the world...' she began and trailed off.

'Tonight you destroyed something innate

inside every woman, something you can never regain or repair. You've coarsened the fiber and I'm glad.'

'Why?' she countered, the flush deepening. In the chill of the early morning dampness her cheeks felt hot.

'You've brought yourself a little nearer down to my level, Miss Randolph, and I am going to treat you accordingly.'

Waldo laughed shortly, displaying yellow, fight-broken teeth in a malevolent grin. 'Have a nice trip, damn you. It'll be the last one you'll ever take, Chann.'

Eric Randolph and his spirited niece led off down the long gentle slope. Pine and fir, sparse here, threw shaggy outlines against the sky.

The great peaks surrounding them, bald up there above timberline, were still snow-capped. Ordway began to shiver uncontrollably. It was more than cold. It was his hands. They were freezing and yet hell's own fire seemed to be pitch-forking through them because Red Waldo had been diabolically vicious with the piggin' string.

He had wanted to make Ordway beg his captors, particularly the girl, for release.

Two miles farther on they crossed a great mesa, broad and grassy in the gray dawn

23

now breaking over the Colorado wilderness. Several times the girl had looked back and now she finally slowed her bay pony until the grulla paced up alongside.

'Are you all right, Mr. Ordway?' she asked with a consideration, bordering upon anxiety.

'Just fine,' he answered stonily. He stared straight ahead. The blood was dry upon his mustache now. The searing agony had crept up into his shoulders, and he could begin to feel it in the back muscles of his neck.

'Again, I'm sorry we didn't divine Red Waldo's intentions. They're an uncouth group of ruffians, but when a determined Scot like my uncle must fight a man such as Ethan Ordway in order to survive there is no choice.'

'I'll be sure to tell Ethan that when I see him today,' he answered.

The sympathy, the apology went out of her. Her full red lips lost their curve and straightened. The bay lunged ahead and pulled up in its proper place again.

Eric Randolph shot his niece a quizzical glance through the steel-rimmed spectacles. 'What's the matter, kitten?' he asked in a low voice. 'Did our bold, bad bandit say something disconcerting.'

'He puzzles me,' she confessed. 'No matter how much I want him to pay with his life for the murder of Wentworth Randolph, he baffles me.'

*    *    *

They entered Squaw Valley shortly after the sun turned the east rim into a golden-edged hedge. The valley was fifteen miles in length and approximately six and a half miles wide; one hundred sections of grass and timberland in total.

Six hundred and forty thousand acres, purchased by an eccentric, world traveling ascetic who had never put a single head of cattle on it. A lot of people, Ordway remembered, wondered why somebody hadn't shot the man and gotten possession. Now it appeared that about the time Channon Ordway left the country for Mexico somebody had.

A great white house with spired turrets like tiny minarets at seven or eight corners loomed ahead. Its construction by workmen brought in from Denver and Cheyenne had at first caused a small amount of awe and then, later, derisive laughter.

Eric Randolph gave the grulla's tether rope to his niece and fell back stirrup-to-stirrup beside Ordway. He gave his prisoner a quizzical smile, his pale eyes sharply etched back of the same kind of spectacles his late brother had worn.

'Quite a place, eh?' he remarked with a wave of his hand. 'Were you ever inside?'

'Only to the front porch,' murmured Ordway. 'Fifteen years ago.'

He was almost beyond pain now. Something was wrong with his vision. He felt as though he'd been drugged. He sat woodenly erect, numb in body and mind, both feet shoved deep into bull-snout *tapaderas*. This alone kept him from falling.

'An architectural monstrosity. Poor old impractical, restive, unhappy Went. I believe that at the time he built it he had some rather vague ideas of becoming a Moslem and converting the rest of America.'

'He was damned handy with that shotgun your niece is carrying,' Ordway heard himself say from far off.

An exceptionally attractive woman of perhaps thirty-eight or forty appeared in

26

the back doorway as they pulled up. There was something of terrible anxiety in her mien as though she had been watching a good part of the night for this return. The manner in which her husband gave smiling reassurance showed he loved her very much.

The ice in his blue eyes had melted into warm sky.

'Mission accomplished without incident, my dear,' he said cheerily. 'Here's the calm, stoical brute who shot poor Went. Hardly less trouble than an uncautious leopard.'

'And the cattle, Eric...' she spoke hesitatingly.

'They're entering the lower end of the valley this moment, Mary. No more trepidations, please. Just some breakfast. Vernell and I are famished and, no doubt, so is our man.'

'Has the sheriff been notified?'

'Sonny will send one of their men before they arrive here and start rebranding in the new corrals.'

He carried the shotgun to his buxom wife, kissed her lightly on the cheek, and came back as the girl dismounted. The complacent grulla lifted its head in answer to a whinny of welcome from two surrey horses in a new corral, then promptly closed its eyes.

Randolph came back and looked up at Ordway. All traces of amiability had vanished. His eyes were blue ice again, his demeanor that of a man used to giving orders and being obeyed.

'Get down,' he ordered curtly. 'I can and will apologize for the beating you suffered. Otherwise you will be fed and held for the arrival of Sheriff Eaton.'

Ordway, however, couldn't move. His legs were dead and the man seemed to be talking from at least a hundred yards away. Impatience and then anger seized Randolph.

'I said for you to dismount!' he snapped.

Slender though he was, the fingers of this transplanted Scot were like blacksmith tongs as he reached up and grabbed Channon Ordway by the left arm. He jerked.

Ordway left the saddle. He fell as a sack falls. He struck hard on his battered face against ground trampled hard by horses' hoofs. A thousand stars exploded into his brain and roared out through his ears.

'Get up, I said!' came the implacable

command. 'I think the brute is faking to gain sympathy.'

Vernell, however, had caught sight of his bound wrists, the thongs sunk deep in swollen flesh. A sharp, piercing cry broke from her.

'Oh, my God, Eric! Look ... his hands. They're swollen and blue! Red Waldo deliberately cut off circulation.'

'By George, you're right,' came the suddenly rueful reply. 'I'm afraid I was a bit rough with the scoundrel. Mary, bring some hot water and cloth. He's bleeding at the mouth again, too.'

Somebody knelt at Ordway's back. A knife blade, cold like a trout's fin, slid in and nicked his skin as it cut the almost hidden piggin' string. It was then that the real agonizing hell of a kind he had never known began to flow through Ordway's battered, bleeding, abused body.

He was only dimly aware of the two pairs of feminine hands working over him. Vernell's were chafing circulation back through his wrists, while those of Mrs. Randolph, using a wet cloth, bathed away the new and dried blood on his unshaved face.

More clearly now, Ordway heard the

older woman's voice in gentle reproof of her husband. 'Eric, it isn't like you to do a thing such as this. Was it necessary to bribe his men to leave, to rob him, to condemn him without giving the man a chance to defend himself? Has this fight against Ethan Ordway, this country itself so soon begun to coarsen you?'

Vernell gave her aunt a startled look across Ordway's lax body. 'Why, that's almost exactly what this man said to me, Aunt Mary.'

Randolph said ruefully: 'Why, I'll apologize to you, my dear. Could I ask you to blame it upon circumstances rather than your husband himself?

He hauled Ordway to his feet and slung an arm around his own neck. The girl, surprisingly strong, did likewise. Half dragging, half carrying him at a stumbling walk, they went into a huge kitchen painted solid white and thence up curving, thickly carpeted stairs. They worked Ordway along a hallway to a huge bedroom facing the south end of Squaw Valley.

They lowered him onto the bed and lifted his feet. The girl then unbuckled and withdrew the bandoleer of cartridges.

'It's so heavy, Eric! But then I suppose a

killer's mind must work with certain logic.'

'Not killer, my dear. Just a hunter who knows how to stalk and down his game.' An exclamation broke from him as he examined the cartridges. 'I say! These are odd-looking cartridges. Not regulation loads at all!'

'No,' Ordway heard her agree as he kept his eyes closed, feigning unconsciousness. 'He needed one of them when he sat his horse at the east veranda and shot poor Wentworth and left him dead in the doorway before riding on to Mexico!'

They crossed to the hallway door and it creaked as she opened it. The room was bright with window-filtered sunlight. The little finger of conscience poking hard at her all day, ever since they had surprised and disarmed him, was hurting her again as she looked in bafflement at the trail-dirty, trail-smelling, fist-battered figure in half-length, heavy leather chaps lying stretched out on the coverlet.

Then a new sound intruded upon the room and the finger touch was gone, replaced by a look of sheer loathing on her aristocratic face with the oddly shaped eyes.

Black Channon Ordway, murderer of her

father, gun fighter, revolutionist from Mexico, and driver-owner of the cattle the Rocking R had taken by guile, was sound asleep.

He was snoring!

The door closed almost with a snap. Ordway opened his one good eye and grinned at the ceiling. Then he rolled over and really did begin to sleep.

He slept the slumber of a man taken pity upon by nature to relieve exhaustion and pain. Hours later when he awoke to the sound of his own driven cattle bawling lustily, new strength had seeped back into his body. So had a gnawing hunger for food.

He lay there for a few moments, clenching and unclenching his hands. The swelling was gone. Except for thong chafe at the wrists his gun hand was as fast as ever. But one thing was certain. He had to get out of here in a hurry, before Step Eaton arrived.

If he ever left this ranch in handcuffs, riding ahead of the man who once before had shot him in the back, he'd never reach Tulac and jail alive.

Step couldn't afford to, and wouldn't, bungle again!

Ordway yawned lustily and sat up, stretching his arms far overhead. He felt good.

Careful not to let his boots thump upon the floor, he eased himself off the bed and to the window. From its two-story height he looked down upon a scene of bustling activity as Sonny and Red Waldo and their men were preparing to start branding Ordway's own cattle.

As he watched, the sound of footsteps ascending from below smote his ears. He quickly stepped back from the window to the bed, sat down, and stretched out full-length on his back once more. He had to close only one eye in full. Red Waldo's savage blow against the point of the cheekbone had done a pretty good job of closing the other.

His breath was coming regularly as in deep slumber when the key grated, the hinges protested from many years of disuse, and two people entered. Two pairs of footsteps cautiously crossed the carpeting, Randolph holding Channon Ordway's own six-shooter.

'Battered and beaten and not a care in the world,' Randolph murmured. 'No conscience in these brutes. Only the basic

33

instincts: live and propagate.'

'It's the only way I can salve my conscience because of the manner in which we have literally stolen his whole herd of cattle,' the girl murmured in reply. 'But you are right, of course, Eric.'

Randolph bent over Ordway and prodded him with the muzzle of his own sequestered .44. But a hand with the speed of a snake's head darted out and snapped the Colt from the surprised Scot. Ordway snapped upright in the bed—and then sheepishly handed back the gun while looking almost into the two bores of the familiar engraved shotgun.

'That's right,' the girl nodded from back of it. 'We take no chances with murderers, Mr. Ordway.'

'Don't blame you a bit,' he grinned, twisting on his rump and lowering his feet to the floor. 'Helps salve the conscience.'

At her angry flush he went on unabashedly: 'It's the glasses. You don't look right without 'em. The Hermit was wearing 'em the day he used that gun on me.'

'He used this weapon on you? Then it's a pity he didn't save his life later by—oh!' she almost stamped her foot on the floor.

'Please get up from there and come downstairs!' This man was *so* exasperating!

She led the way and with Ordway between them, his own gun at his back, they started down. The peso spur rowels made odd rolling sounds as they descended the curved stairs.

The girl spoke back over her shoulder. 'I am at least pleased that your male vanity prevents your spur rowels from tearing at the carpeting. It was imported from China.'

'These spurs, ma'am?' he drawled at the back of her slender neck below a copper-colored hair bun. 'They're not mine, really. I stole 'em off the feet of a dead Mexican general after I killed him in a box canyon fight just west of Parral, in the state of Chihuahua.'

A disdainful sniff came audibly. Her lips compressed as she made a mental note not to speak with the brute again. He had a way of getting back at her and seemingly enjoying himself at her expense.

At the bottom of the stairs, however, he blandly ignored the guns and went over to a window, where he bent down and peered through at the corrals and cattle and the herd out beyond. To her amazement he began to chuckle over something he seemed

35

to find vastly amusing.

'You find it amusing that we've stolen your cattle and are rebranding them?' she demanded contentiously despite her self-promise of but moments ago.

'A little,' he chuckled. He straightened and grinned at her out of one good eye. 'You see, ma'm *I* stole 'em too.'

She gave her uncle a baffled look, a question in her own eyes. Randolph said imperturbably: 'What he probably means, my dear, is that he first shot poor old Went to obtain the valley. He likely intends now to succeed where his notorious family associate, Ethan Ordway, failed; that is, take over our brand too.'

Her eyes surveyed Ordway mockingly. 'Is that true?' she smiled.

'Not all of it, ma'm,' he answered gravely. 'I was born during a bad snowstorm, in a Ute Indian tepee, on about the spot where you built those new branding chutes to rebrand my herd. My godfather, an old fellow called White Buffalo, told my mother that one day this valley would be mine.'

'And you believed all this . . . this pagan prophesy to the extent of killing an elderly recluse.'

'I believed only that part of it,' he answered quietly. His voice turned cool, devoid now of the drawl she knew he used only when he mocked her.

'You see, Miss Randolph, there was more. It also was said that I'd find myself a beautiful white squaw here. But there is a girl in Tulac named Kathy Perry with whom I'm very much in love. So I really couldn't find myself a white squaw, now could I? Will you lead the way . . . *ma'm?*'

From her position over a hot stove Mary Randolph gave Ordway a smile that was a mixture of regret, sadness, and trepidation. But there was welcome, too, and a place for one had been set at a table where exquisite silverware gleamed against a snowy tablecloth and napkin.

She said gently, 'If you'd care to finish my rather awkward efforts to cleanse your poor battered face, Mr. Ordway, I'll have your food ready.'

He gave her a reassuring smile and went to a sink equipped with cistern hand pump. On a shelf above it was a photo of three smiling boys, ages about eleven, thirteen, and fourteen. Imps all, from their looks.

'Yours?' he asked, soaping his hands in the pan of warm water.

She nodded. 'They're in school abroad. We'll bring them here next year. Were there others in your own immediate family?'

He said, 'Yes, Mrs. Randolph,' and bent over to soap his face and swollen left eye.

He finished his ablutions while the girl and her uncle stood apart, silent and aloof. Ordway took a comb from a pocket of the bolero jacket and put his dark hair in order.

'Do you feel better now?' Mrs. Randolph inquired.

'Physically, yes,' he said. 'But if I were you, I'd remove that photo of the boys to another place.'

'Oh?'

'Yes, ma'm,' Channon Ordway answered her. 'You see, because of what your husband and niece have done to me today I'm going to burn out the Rocking R and take over the valley, Indian-named after my mother and my birth here in a tepee. And because of your kindness, and those three boys there on the shelf, I'm going to do it with a certain sense of regret.'

# CHAPTER THREE

In a strained silence broken only by the suddenly increased bawls of cattle under stamping irons in the two eight-cow branding chutes, Channon Ordway sat down to eat in the house he had calmly informed the occupants he intended to burn. He placed a napkin across his chapped legs and with consummate skill used silver knife and fork to cut into the juicy roast. He began to eat.

He became aware that the girl was watching him with growing puzzlement and, perhaps, a somewhat clearer understanding of his background. And this would never do. There was a heaping portion of creamed potatoes on the chinaware plate and Ordway used the knife.

He shoved it deep under the pile, lifted it, and transferred the whole of the load into his mouth. When he belched, the girl could take no more of his coarse baiting. She fled the room and he didn't dare look at Mrs. Randolph, for whom he was beginning to have a deep respect.

She apparently felt that her husband and niece were wrong, probably had argued against their violently arbitrary action and the risk of disarming a noted killer on the way home from Mexico. But there was no question of where her blind love and loyalty positioned her: she'd stand by Randolph and the girl to the last glowing ember in a burned house built by an eccentric.

Ordway finished the meal and started to use the napkin but thought better of it. When his handkerchief came away from his mouth it was spotted with red. The first-made cuts had broken open again.

'I am so sorry,' she murmured as he rose and pushed back.

'Don't be,' he told her gently. 'My own mother would have said that sometimes these things simply happen. She married my outlaw father and reformed him. You married one with too much stubborn, foolish pride.'

Eric Randolph's face remained coldly aloof, his mouth Scot-stubborn. He gave a curt nod, backed up by Ordway's .44 Colt, and they walked through two more rooms before emerging into a great living room fronted by a long veranda enclosed by figured railing. Here were bookshelves from floor to ceiling, a varnished ladder to get at the high ones, a massive, paper-covered secretary where Randolph apparently conducted his correspondence, and a glassed-in case containing thirty or forty rifles and pistols.

One of the rifles was a single-shot .45-70 and the bandoleer of long cartridges draped on a peg beside it was all too familiar. Eric Randolph obviously considered Ordway as good as dead, and the thought angered the prisoner.

The rancher said, 'If you'll be seated, Vernell will bring coffee. Although it undoubtedly means little to you, sir, she feels very unhappy over the matter of Red Waldo, binding your wrists too tight and our negligence in failing to take precautions for your comfort.'

He indicated a leather chair and himself took seat in a large settee, also of leather. Randolph waved the pistol. 'Make yourself comfortable until the sheriff arrives. He and one of the hands who hurried to Tulac will be here in a few minutes.'

'I expect Step will be right glad to see me,' Ordway replied dryly, as Vernell came in with two cups of black coffee. 'We were such good *compadres* ever since we were

41

kids.'

'And you are hoping that it will make some difference in the final discharge of his duties as an officer of the law?' she asked acidly.

'Oh, no, ma'm!' he protested vigorously. 'You got my word Step won't let me get away. Not him!'

She was still antagonistically puzzled over that remark when the sheriff finally arrived. One horse loped on past the spired mansion to the corrals, where its rider excitedly reported to Sonny and Red Waldo at the branding chutes. The other horse, a gleaming black mare with racing lines, came to a halt at about the spot where a mounted man presumably had sat his saddle and shot Wentworth Randolph to death in his front doorway.

A man firing a .45-70-500 Sharps rifle.

Ignoring Eric Randolph's freezing command backed up by the Colt, Ordway got to his feet and glanced out the front window. Step Eaton, much heavier and unhealthily florid of face from too much steady drinking, was tying the black mare's reins to a veranda support. In keeping with his new tenure as sheriff, he wore black suit and white shirt, string tie and white

Stetson.

No doubt about it, Ordway thought, Step had really been living it up with that fifteen thousand he'd taken as Ordway lay bleeding and unconscious from the cowardly shot in the back.

Step jauntily crossed the porch and banged a *shave-and-a-haircut* (pause) *two-bits* on the eight-foot-tall French doors. With this to announce his presence and humming a gay tune, he opened the door and came in too late to heed Eric Randolph's sudden warning cry. He had stepped squarely into fist range of a man he'd left for dead fifteen months ago.

One of Ordway's hands snapped Step's pistol from the holster beneath the coat of gleaming black broadcloth. The other, balled into a iron fist, smashed the sheriff alongside the head and sent him reeling a dozen feet. Step Eaton hit the leather settee and sat down heavily beside the startled Randolph.

Ordway stood facing them, legs braced apart, Step's cocked gun in his deadly capable right hand. His black eyes above the mustache and whiskers bored mercilessly into the panic-stricken ones of Eaton.

'Chann...' the sheriff whispered chokingly, face already dead.

'With no apologies for feminine company present, what have you got to say in the one minute you have left to live, you back-shooting, money-robbing, son-of-a-bitch?' Ordway asked with rising fury.

'Chann...' It came in a final, desperate, choked whisper.

He couldn't finish. A pocket of air, musk-tasting, had lodged spastically somewhere in his constricted throat. He swallowed hard in an attempt to regain speech, to stall off death as terror of death mounted. A muscle quivered beneath a chin, left barber-slick and with an odor of fermented roses. 'Chann ... I ... Chann...'

Randolph said cuttingly, tossing Ordway's pistol, 'Here. I can't turn you over to such a coward.' Acting as though he hadn't heard, Channon Ordway looked down at what appeared to be the girl's legs. A second time now, she thought. In his savage rage and hatred he's still baiting a woman.

Now he stepped back and tossed the sheriff's gun into the black-trousered lap. 'Get up, Step,' he ordered. 'As long as these arrogantly bungling, ineptly proud people figure I killed their looney relative who peppered me and my pony in the back one day, killing another man in their bat-infested temple won't make a great deal of difference. Get up and use the gun, you would-be murdering scum.'

Eaton, however, made no move to touch his pistol. His eyes, dulled by shocking, numbing fear of death, looked up in mute appeal to the grim apparition. 'Shoot if you want,' he choked huskily. 'I won't.'

Ordway stepped over and took his rifle and bandoleer from the glass-enclosed gun rack. He slung the weight of the big cartridges over his shoulder and buckled. He stood like death itself over the cringing figure of the man he'd known when they were children and their fathers rode the outlaw trails together long before that.

He said harshly: 'Did somebody pay you to shoot me in the back and take that cattle-buying money, Step, or did you think of it all by yourself?'

But again he was met by mute silence and a shake of the head that might have meant anything.

He turned to the girl. 'Go bring my grulla horse to the back door without arousing suspicion of Sonny's outfit out there branding my cattle. The way I feel right now I won't wait until later to burn down the Hermit's insane eyesore. I'll torch it before I go.'

'I fully believe that,' she answered coolly, 'and I'll do my best.'

'No double-cross?'

'I said I'll do my best,' she answered and left them.

In the kitchen she held up an admonishing finger to her lips to enjoin silence from her aunt and made her way to the surrey team corral. The grulla, fed and well rested, already had made itself at home. It stood hipshot with mouse-colored chin resting in equine camaraderie over the rump of one of the span.

But when she approached it with Ordway's bridle the wary grulla came alive fast and spun away. To her great, almost panicky dismay, she was discovering that there was much difference in the training of a range mount from that of the buggy team. This one not only would not accept the bridle, it demanded to be roped.

'And that man Ordway knew it too, I suspect!' she told herself fiercely.

This left but one choice. She gingerly

took down Ordway's rawhide reata of stiffened coils from the cactus-tree fork of the flathorn Mexican saddle. In her anger she noticed the mirror fastened to the top of the flathorn and automatically surmised that, like other *caballeros*, he used it to preen himself as he rode along. Then she remembered how he had acquired his boots and silver spurs with the peso rowels and she didn't know who to be angry at: Ordway or herself.

The reata was iron hard to her hands and after a few awkward tries, which the grulla easily dodged, she stood in the center of the corral, feeling helpless for the first time in her life. She had hunted with Eric since the time, so many years ago, he had found her in Burma where Wentworth Randolph had abandoned her Eurasian mother. She'd mothered his and Mary's three wildcat sons while they were gone. She had . . .

'Oh, damn!' she angrily exclaimed.

'Havin' trouble?' inquired a bland voice that was positively infuriating.

Red Waldo, unseen, had climbed the pole fence and dropped to the ground, and was waddling toward her like a fat Indian buck. Unknown to her, he had given Sonny a significant wink before leaving the chutes.

'Quite obviously I am, Mr. Waldo,' she answered coolly.

'Anything ol' Reddie kin do?'

'Yes. Please lasso that mount belonging to Mr. Ordway.'

'Now how come Mister Ordway didn't come out here to the lot an' lasso that hoss hisself?' he demanded with little glints of suspicion in his red-rimmed eyes.

'I would think you could guess. His hands were swollen after the manner in which you trussed them. Deliberately, I suspect.'

'Hands all swole, huh?' he said thoughtfully, and a hidden gleam brightened lashless orbs. 'Pore Boy. Here. Gimme.'

He built a loop with a flick of his hairy wrist, and with another flick he roped the grulla. It came forward meekly and made no protest as the heavy saddle and bull-snout taps thumped over its short coupled back. He hauled up and notched the latigo leather.

'There,' Waldo grinned at her, handing over the reins. 'You couldn't a caught him with a bridle in a month of Sundays. Cow hoss pride. You orta learn how to throw a rope.'

'Just give me a little time to practice after today, Mr. Waldo, and I assure you I'll need not again call upon anyone for assistance.'

'Y'know, I don't think you will either, lady,' he admitted with rare grudging admiration.

He stood watching as she closed the gate and led the grulla toward the back of the towering white house so much like a miniature castle of wood instead of stone. Everybody in the whole country had known from the beginning that there was something wrong with the man who had built it, and odd about the house itself. Take now how the Hermit had peppered twelve-year-old Chann Ordway in the back that time, Waldo remembered.

Everything wrong about all these people. Must be something plenty wrong in that house right now, too, Red told himself.

He wheeled and strode to the pole fence, climbed it swiftly for a man of his squat, build, and dropped to the ground once more. He hurried over to one of the eight-cow branding chutes, now jammed with bawling cattle. A branding fire was going good, with a tender watching a cluster of

49

Rocking R stamping irons made in Denver.

Sonny deftly stamped the last of his four in the chute in a way his rustler father would have approved, came out of the pungent cloud of smoke, gave the iron tender a contemptuous look.

'I coulda done better with a heated cinch ring between two holding sticks right on the open range,' he sneered, and wiped a sleeve across his ruggedly handsome young face.

He pushed back his long blond locks and rearranged his hat.

'Sonny,' Red Waldo said.

'What's with that high falutin' filly? I'd like to get my hands on her someday.'

'She allows as Chann's hands are all swole up on account of the way I tied his wrists with piggin' string,' grinned Waldo. 'She allows as how I was so cruel it wasn't accident-like at all,' he winked.

'That how come she saddled his hoss?' Sonny demanded suspiciously.

'Uh-huh. But how come you reckon Eric an' Step didn't just bring along the prisoner, and one of them do it?'

Sonny bent suddenly and grasped the dangling ends of the thongs in the tip of his gun sheath. He had untied them from around his legs to give full freedom while working the stamping iron.

'Maybe I'd better go have a look-see,' he said thinly.

'No,' his pardner corrected. 'Maybe *I* better go have a look-see. When Chann killed my brother in Cheyenne that was bad enough. But when he shot a good hoss from under me with that bloomin' Sharps cannon . . .'

He shifted his gun sheath into place at one heavy hip. 'And besides, didn't the gal say as how his hands was all swole up to where he cain't use 'em?'

He circled a corral and, under cover, began an approach toward the front veranda where Step Eaton's racing mare made a black sheen against the railing.

Sonny watched him go, grinning. They'd taken an awful drubbing back there a few weeks ago when, under Ethan's orders, they'd tried to take the herd. One man killed and horses shot from under Red and two others.

Then, to their and Ethan's laughter, this Randolph dude had hunted them up and *hired them to do the same job!*

# CHAPTER FOUR

At the rear of the house, Vernell left the grulla ground-tied. If the stubborn animal had enough 'hoss pride' that it could be caught only by the use of a lasso, then it certainly wouldn't move as long as the reins lay on the ground.

She re-entered the kitchen. Her aunt had just turned from the shelf over the sink, with a framed photo of three boys in her hands. 'Why, Aunt Mary, what on earth,' the girl exclaimed. 'Surely you don't believe—'

'The manner in which Eric is recovering the same number of cattle stolen by Ethan Ordway frightens me, Vernell. Now we've made a second enemy more terrible than the first.'

'You really believe he'll try to burn us out?'

'He doesn't strike me as a man of idle boasts. And when he learns that Kathy Perry believed him dead and married Sheriff Eaton during his absence I shudder to think what may happen.'

'I suppose you're right,' sighed the girl.

'Even that could hurt an unregenerate brute. At least there is *something* that can hurt him!'

She strode determinedly back into the great living room. Ordway now stood easily as though there wasn't an enemy within miles instead of exactly one dozen of them within a hundred and fifty yards. He was speaking sardonically to the deflated sheriff as Vernell came in.

'So you took the money off me and went ahead and bought a herd with it anyhow, huh? Didn't have nerve to come back loaded with cash and try to lie to Ethan. He'd have taken the hide off you.'

Step remained silent.

'You took fifteen thousand off me, bought a Mexican herd at ten dollars a head, and came home,' Ordway pressed relentlessly. 'What happened to it?'

'Fattened on Pronghorn grass and sold in Cheyenne by your uncle,' Vernell interrupted. 'And now, your unbathed Excellency, your horse awaits.'

'Any trouble?' He had to grin despite Step's presence. This girl had spunk!

'You overestimated my ability with a lasso,' she replied icily. 'Red Waldo saddled the horse for me, and asked questions . . . you fool!'

'Thank you for the warning.' He spoke a final grim word to the sheriff: 'Step, I'll find out why Tobe Whitehouse had to die, why Koonce is still wearing a badge under you. And when we meet again, you will be paid three bullets in front for two through my back.'

Eaton started to speak. But his eyes widened, looking past Ordway, and Channon spun toward the front doors. One had opened noiselessly. In the opening stood Red Waldo with a big pistol in his right hand. His red-rimmed eyes, many years lashless, from Harridan disease, were flat, dead.

'My brother Jude Waldo tried an even break and got killed. I had to wait for this. Here goes fer him and a good hoss you shot out from under me at six hundred yards.'

Vernell never saw Ordway's hand make the draw. In less than a second, she heard the ear-ringing thunder of the .44, and then again. Red Waldo staggered backward through the doorway to the porch edge. His shoulders struck the gallery support to which the shiny black mare was tied.

The high-strung animal shrilled, reared. Broken reins gave a snapping sound. She fled away with head held high, looking back in fright.

Dying, Waldo reflexed a bullet through Ordway's sombrero brim, and then that was all; the end of a life of theft, murder, rape and brutality.

Without emotion, the man robbed of his herd shot Waldo again.

Red Waldo's body fell slackly in an ugly heap like a sack of grain thrown on its side and bent slightly at the thick, tight-pressed middle. The black mare stopped running, one hundred yards away, and now stood facing the ranch, blowing loudly, trembling, broken reins dangling.

Vernell saw it all through horrified eyes riveted mainly upon a pair of worn boots with run down heels, hanging by the sharp toes from the edge of the porch. The rest of the man's toad-shaped body, slain lightning fast, lay in the dirt, with a stream of bright crimson flowing from flabby lips slacking around a cruel mouth.

When Channon Ordway turned, black eyes brittle, she knew even before he spoke to Eric almost what his words would be. 'The only reason that didn't happen to you when we met, Randolph, was because I figured you for an outlandish greenhorn who just didn't know any better. Otherwise, I'd have dropped you.'

He strode back to where she stood, pushed her aside. He bent swiftly to a thick, dusty volume of the bottom shelf, right on the carpeting where her ankles had been.

He straightened with the book in one hand, and spoke dismissingly to the girl. 'Your legs, Miss Randolph? I've seen prettier. Kath Perry's, for instance. I was looking at a bullet hole in the back of this book.'

He opened a large volume, leather bound. Plato. In the center pages, like a snug, rain-colored cocoon, buried against a barricade of torn, smashed, accordion-shaped folds of philosophy written centuries before, lay a big bullet. Channon Ordway handed her the opened book.

'It probably was fired by a man sitting at the front porch astride his horse. It passed through your father's body as he stood in the doorway. Slanted down and lodged into this book.'

He faced Eric Randolph, his eyes turning scathingly angry. 'You're supposed to be an intelligent man, not to mention a gun expert. Weigh that bullet. I own the only five-hundred-grain Sharps in this country.

I inherited it from my father. Most of his outlaw friends preferred repeaters: Henrys, Spencers, Winchester Seventy-threes.'

He moved toward the kitchen, turned for one savage thrust at them. 'If I'd have wanted to kill the Hermit, I'd have done it long ago: after the day I rode over here with a note from Ethan to buy out this place and he peppered me in the back with that shotgun you're so handy with, Miss Randolph. I was twelve years old and my mother had just died.'

In the kitchen he saw Mrs. Randolph with the picture of her sons still in her hands. Running footsteps were converging toward the front. He said, 'I'm sorry they'll have no place to come to, Mrs. Randolph.'

'There was death in this house before you came, Mr. Ordway. The death of a man's disintegrating soul after he absconded with much of the Randolph family fortune. Go, now. Hurry. I feel in my heart that we've wronged you.'

He plunged through the kitchen door and down the two steps, and was up fast into the Mexican saddle. Several men, led by Sonny, were running toward the front. One of them spotted Ordway and foolishly clawed out his pistol, giving a yell of warning.

The .45–70 in Ordway's hands snapped up to his shoulder. The vicious kick came with the lethal buffalo killer's throaty roar. Seventy grains of black powder drove five hundred grains of lead slug into a man, and killed him.

The grulla exploded into pumping movement and slammed northward up the length of the valley toward the north end; the north promontory where the old outlaws in an unnamed settlement used to watch for the coming of the lawmen.

The chunky grulla did a magnificent job of eating up the six miles, galloping and trotting by turns. There was no pursuit; not in the face of a rifle that reached a long way out and struck with the weight of a sledgehammer. Ordway would have bet that the black mare ridden by Step had had enough for today.

His nerve was gone. What he would need would be a few big drinks, preferably undiluted. He'd wait, and likely ride in with Sonny.

Ordway came to the upper end of the valley with the strange name, and began a slow ascent of the road leading up to the promontory and the town there. Once upo.

a time Eric Randolph, comparatively new in the valley, had asked Ethan Ordway the reason why Bitter Squaw had been so named.

'And do you know,' he later confided to Mike Adkins in Mike's bank, 'I thought the scoundrel was going to draw his revolver and strike at my head.'

Ordway reached the top. The grulla gave a satisfied heave of its barrel and latigo leather ceased to creak. Ahead of them was a line of log structures built in the days when the fathers of Channon Ordway, Step Eaton, Sonny Shackleford, Robert Koonce, the deputy sheriff, and Kathy Perry had to watch for both the law and the warlike Ute Indians.

Thoughts of Kathy sent a warm feeling through Ordway as he rode toward the low, broad structure built by Hansen, another of the old bunch.

He knew the whole town must be aware of his coming. Step would have told it over a few drinks before departing south to the Rocking R to 'bring in' his prisoner. Half the town had likely viewed Ordway's progress up the valley.

Now he was here, back from the dead after fifteen months, and somewhere along the line there were questions to be answered. Somewhere along the line more men were going to die.

It was typical that nobody was on Hansen's porch when Channon Ordway arrived. Too many were from the old days. They'd be inside, studiously careful and trying to act surprised when he entered.

As Ordway dismounted a man came backing out of the doorway, shoved by a bigger man's hand. Lon Perry, Kathy's father, was a bit unsteady on his feet. He was followed by the gaunt, towering, black-browed figure of scowling Ethan Ordway.

Lon made a pitiable effort to regain lost dignity. He said, 'Ethan, there was a time in the old days when you would have needed a gun to do this. Sure, I'm a boozed-out shell now, but...'

'Get on back to the livery where you're paid to work,' growled Ethan. 'I'm tired of you loafing and bumming drinks.'

He looked at Channon. There was no surprise or welcome, and certainly no affection in his mien. He always had been a dark, brooding man. He now divided his time between the ranch in Pronghorn Basin, a short distance east, and living quarters in town, near the livery he owned.

It might have been ten minutes instead of more than a year, from the manner in which he greeted his nephew, without handshake. 'I heard you were coming back with a herd. Pronghorn's empty.'

'Thanks,' Ordway replied dryly. 'Some other people seem to have heard, too. I'm just wondering if you knew that also.'

He turned to Lon Perry and extended his hand. 'Good to see you again, Lon.'

They shook. The older man wore a haggard look beyond the ravages of whiskey-raw nerves. His eyes were pleading with Channon about something.

Ordway said, 'I'm expecting some trouble with the sheriff and likely some new "deputies" comprising Sonny's outfit, Lon. Take the grulla over and saddle me the best horse Ethan has. Leave him in front of the courthouse.'

'You got to leave again? You maybe wing Step—'

'No.'

'I wish to God you'd killed him!' Perry burst out. 'Chann, there's something I got to tell you—'

'I don't discuss Kathy in the street in front of a saloon, Lon,' Ordway said almost curtly. 'Later. Just bring the horse.'

61

Perry mumbled a shamefaced apology and, with a bit of difficulty, mounted the grulla and rode west along the curve of the old fort to the sprawling livery over there in an open space all to itself. Ordway walked past his uncle and went inside. In the days when Channon's reformed outlaw father and his gentle-bred mother lived in the Basin, and Ethan, as pardner, shared table and house, he'd shown no interest in the boy he couldn't dominate. At least nothing visible. He'd been almost covert at times.

He showed a little more now, however. He followed his nephew, and his black, Ordway eyes were a little harder, a little more speculative than usual.

Twice now, Step had bungled. He'd failed to make the kill in Mexico but had been somewhat forgiven when word came that Ordway was not dead at all but on the way home with a bigger herd.

But today he'd done it again. He was supposed to have left the Rocking R with his prisoner and made certain Channon never reached Tulac alive. But... Where was that damned bottle-slugging fool now?

Ordway shook hands with Hansen. As an outlaw Hanse had built his first cabin over two tree stumps, nailed a hand sawed board between them, and started business with a five gallon keg of Indian trader whiskey.

'Glad to see you back,' he rumbled, and returned to business.

Mike Adkins, prematurely white-haired, was a medium built man whose flair for letting money stick to his fingers in the old outlaw days had landed him in his own bank. It was he who had loaned Channon and Ethan the money used on a cattle buying trip which had left Channon for dead.

Ordway said, 'Mike, come in the back room with Ethan and me. I want to ask a few questions.'

Mike shot an uneasy glance at Ethan before he caught himself. He'd known Channon since the day Doc Cartwright had planned to deliver him, except that Doc had been caught in a snowstorm and couldn't get there.

Mike shook his head. 'Plenty of time, Chann. Family stuff first. Business later.'

'All right, Mike, but this happens to *be* business.'

He turned to the towering man above the bar, who was taller by an inch or so than even Ethan. 'Hanse, give me a bottle and glasses. If Step comes in—he shot me in the

63

back in Mexico and robbed me—tell him where I am?'

'You didn't kill him? I'm glad.'

'Why?'

'He's been loaded with money since he came home with a herd and that yarn about you getting hit in a revolution. But he lost it on high living and a black racing mare. He owes me money.'

'If he gets his nerve back you won't collect,' Ordway said grimly.

Several men shot him strange looks which Ordway did not understand, and even Hanse looked queer. What the devil was wrong with them anyhow?

In the rear room Ordway placed bottle and glasses and pitcher on the green-topped poker table. He removed his sombrero and sat down. Ethan's dark eyes were sneeringly sardonic as he looked over his long absent nephew's raiment and followed suit.

'Step said you'd gone native down there,' he remarked and unstoppered the bottle by working his thumb against the top. 'Looks like he was right.'

'Gringos make too good a target in the midst of several hundred men in a horseback fight. And "No sabe" saved much bother on the drive here.'

'What do you plan to do?'

'Find some answers,' Ordway answered bluntly.

A green fly, harbinger of spring, buzzed against a rear window where a year before there had been nothing but privies, empty bottles and years of trash accumulation. Buckskin clad mountain-trappers first had wintered here in shelters of brush and skins, keeping wary eyes out for Utes.

Later came the outlaws, one by one, good men and bad, who discovered that the location was ideal to spot the approach of lawmen coming up the valley from the south or through the huge basin to the east.

Now there was a graded square around a flat topped little courthouse. Tulac was growing civilized.

The fly buzzed again and with a grunt of annoyance Ethan got up and killed it with a newspaper. 'Never could stand the damned things inside a house,' he explained.

No, Ordway thought, nor did you ever bother to explain your actions to any man, least of all a nephew you've hated all your life. Ethan sat down again and drank.

'So you want some answers. Suppose you tell me first what happened down in

Mexico.'

Ordway, thinking of Sonny's outfit coming up the valley, talked swiftly.

He told the cadaverous-faced man across the table how Step had shot him in the back one day and fled with the money Channon and Ethan had borrowed from Mike Adkins. He told of some outlawed *vaqueros* who found him almost dead from loss of blood; how after months of convalescence he joined their revolutionary movement.

'It's a good way to die quick if you lose or take your pay in loot and become rich if you win. We won—at least long enough that I got out with two thousand head of cattle.'

'How come you brought them back here to give me a half share?'

Channon Ordway was almost taken aback. He nearly stared at his uncle. His voice hardened. 'You probably won't believe it, Ethan, but I felt that I'd let Mike down. I wanted to make certain he got paid, that we didn't lose Pronghorn should Mike have got too far out on a limb and had to foreclose.'

'He didn't,' Ethan said grimly.

'I know,' Channon Ordway nodded. 'Step drove back a herd for you and then accepted a few morsels such as money and a racing mare you tossed from the table. After you sold our cattle in Cheyenne.'

'He got a little more than that,' Ethan grinned with something evil and unclean in it. 'He got Kathy Perry, who thought you were dead.'

'He married Kathy?' Ordway asked incredulously. He couldn't believe this. Then he remembered what Lon Perry had tried to tell him a few moments ago, the looks on the faces of the men at the bar when he spoke of killing Step. They had known. Maybe they had pitied him a little.

Channon Ordway rose to his feet. 'This was all your doing, Ethan,' he said coldly. 'The Hermit dead, Tobe Whitehouse dead and Step wearing his badge. Since Step was a kid here in town he never went to the privy without first asking you!'

An abrupt knock came at the door. It opened. Hanse's huge white head and fiercely unswept Prussian mustaches appeared. 'Visitors, Chann,' he announced.

'How far down the valley, Hanse?'

'Not far enough for you. And my long-glass says only Step and Sonny are in front. Not a sign of Red Waldo.'

'You getting old—butting in on something?' Ethan demanded harshly.

Hanse said to Ordway: 'Red's an awful sneaky man with a rifle, Chann.' He ignored Ethan's scowling threat.

'Not anymore,' Ordway answered grimly. 'Waldo is dead. I killed him down at the Randolph Ranch, on about the spot in the doorway where somebody killed the Hermit the day I left for Mexico.'

'Good,' Hansen grunted in satisfaction.

He pulled back and the door closed once more.

Ordway turned his attention back to his wary uncle. 'And Randolph's Rocking R cattle, Ethan? You stole them all, didn't you? The whole country must surely know that. Yet not a man will speak up because they're afraid of you. Even Mike wouldn't come in and talk.'

He paused in the face of Ethan's silence, but no answer came. He said almost softly: 'You never reformed, did you, Ethan? You never wanted to because you are a man born without a conscience.'

# CHAPTER FIVE

There was no immediate reaction, no expected explosion of a violent temper across the table. Ethan was a man who lived in his own dark world. He masked his thoughts and brooked no outside interference.

Looking now at his giant uncle, Ordway thought: *When mother had her choice of Tim and him and chose Tim, Ethan should have found a wife elsewhere. A good woman, patient enough to remain silent during his black moods. Strong like my mother when Tim became restive for the old days.*

*But he never got over it, never stopped hating, and I've often wondered what really happened the night I was born.*

*Doc Cartwright had been standing by in Tulac, expecting the call most any day or night. But a bad snowstorm had come up that night, and Doc had answered another similar call to a trapper's cabin. By the time Tim Ordway got to him they were both snowed in.*

*Yet sometime before the storm reached its full-throated fury, Ellen Ordway had left the ranch, slipping away from it and Ethan, and only by the grace of God and an Indian pony given her by White Buffalo had she stumbled into the little Ute camp in the valley and borne her son in the friendly old man's tepee.*

Channon Ordway, his face still bearing the black marks of the beating, brought himself back to the present. 'The answers, Ethan. I'm waiting. From the day I left here you never intended for me to get back alive, did you? You killed the Hermit and laid the blame on me, even as you took possession of the valley where I was born in a tepee. When I wrote Kathy I was on the way home—very much alive—you sent Sonny and his outfit south to finish the job and take my herd. They took a bad licking. How many years have you planned all this, Ethan? Since the day after my mother was buried and you sent me to Squaw Valley, thinking the Hermit might kill me?'

Ethan Ordway's eyes changed. They began to glow like black coals. He placed two huge hands, fingers spread, upon the table top. His arms and elbows were out as though he would push himself erect like a tower of strength and anger in the back room.

He remained that way as he looked into Ordway's battered face and one good eye.

Yet his voice held a peculiarly restrained quality as he spoke.

'You want some answers, you'll get them!'

A deep breath filled his lungs and sighed out once more. 'It was just thirty years ago this month when Tim and me came into this country on the dodge and settled. He wanted to turn straight and ranch, but the land we wanted, Pronghorn Basin, was so full of soddy dugouts it looked like a prairie-dog town.

'If it had been left up to your father we'd never have got Pronghorn. He was too softhearted.'

Ordway said, 'We both know that. That was why my mother chose him instead of you. It's why you hated me from the day I was born and her until the day she died.'

'Listen to me!' Ethan almost thundered. 'It was my gun and a necessary ruthlessness that cleared the basin and made it ours. That's why from the day he died I considered everything as mine.'

'He gave his life for you in this very saloon. He sacrificed himself because you were caught in a three-way gun brace.'

'It makes no difference! Pronghorn was mine from that day and I only tolerated your ma because she wouldn't leave when I ordered her to.'

Unmoved, holding his own terrible killing urge under control, Ordway said: 'You treated her everyday the same way I treated that Randolph girl today and for the same reason: to cover up the fact that she was too far above you.'

It was true about Vernell Randolph. In this respect, Ordway knew, he was little better than an uncle who for years ignored the napkin Ellen Ordway placed by Ethan's plate each meal.

In this respect Ordway had gone him one better. He'd used his knife to shovel in potatoes. In her hearing he'd called Step a back-shooting son-of-a-bitch. And before her horrified eyes he had shot a man three times and killed him.

Ordway looked across at his uncle. Their drinks were forgotten. This could be a shootout. Or could he bring himself to down Tim's brother?

'You have categorically admitted the ugly truth, Ethan,' he stated. 'You waited all these years for Step and Sonny to grow up. You planned everything—maybe including Tim's death, didn't you?— *because you never got over my mother!*'

'I've heard enough!' Ethan shouted and pushed back from the table. His eyes were wild beneath his shaggy black hair still unstreaked with gray.

'Ethan,' Channon Ordway went on in a terrible voice almost trembling with pent-up passion, *'why did my mother flee from you and the ranch the night I was born?'*

Now Ethan Ordway came to his feet. The room seemed to shrink, so big did he tower in it. He bent forward at the waist and placed his doubled fists on the table and rested himself on long, elbow-locked arms. His face was a frightful thing to see.

'I'm through talking! Get on that fresh horse and ride out before Sonny and Step get here. It's your only chance to stay alive!'

'Not until I get an answer, Ethan!'

'You'll get an answer in hell where she went,' Ethan Ordway almost screamed. 'You're only half Ordway anyhow. She diluted your blood and made you a—'

He never finished the rest of it, for Channon Ordway almost exploded over the table at him, six-shooter up and out. Ethan had tried only once to whip him, about a year after Ellen Ordway was buried in the basin. Channon had swung the pole-ax in a

73

flash and by a hair-breadth missed splitting Ethan's skull.

Now, after fourteen years, Channon Ordway swung again at his uncle's head.

The barrel lashed out in a thudding side swipe. Ethan crashed forward and the table tipped at a crazy angle and then skidded and fell over. Ordway, his one good eye flaming, landed on top of the giant.

The barrel of the .44 began to thud down into Ethan's upturned face the way Red Waldo's iron fists had thudded into Channon's own battered countenance. Soddenly. Cruelly. Again and again. Ordway against black Ordway.

Channon finally came to his feet and stood panting more from anger than exertion. He sheathed the gun and stood looking down at a bleeding mass of bruised flesh who had just undergone a masterful job of pistol whipping.

Ethan groaned, rolled over and half propped himself up on an elbow. He spat a stream of blood and then used his fingers to extract a loose tooth.

'Finish me ... while you have the chance,' he slobbered in a whisper. 'You'll never get another ... before you die!'

The door re-opened and Hanse came in.

His face was imperturbable, as usual. Few things bothered this close-mouthed, white-headed giant.

'As I told Henry Cartwright the other day—him and Mike Adkins,' Hanse growled and bent over Ethan's recumbent form, 'I liked it better in the old days.'

He rolled Ethan onto his back, stood at his head and secured a grip under both armpits. He brought up the giant with ease, shifted him over to one arm like a child, and picked up the overturned chair and table.

'You just shot a man, and his friends either dealt themselves a hand or packed him out,' Hanse went on as he sat Ethan in the chair and let him fall forward with his face bloodying the green table. 'No fuss, no feathers.'

He poured whiskey into a palm like a grizzly's claw, flung Ethan's head back, smeared his smashed face and ignored the foul curses of pain.

'Now you got to treat 'em like babies,' he growled and went to the door. There he turned. 'I'll send for Henry Cartwright to take care of him, Chann. Now you get out of here and have old Pete next door use some leeches to get that other eye of yours

75

open before Sonny gets here.'

Ordway sheathed his gun and stepped through the rear door onto a new porch, one of several which had been added to the rears of buildings formerly facing nothing but desertion and trash. He ducked past a striped barber pole and stuck his head through and spoke to the dour-visaged individual who looked as though he'd been sucking a chunk of alum most of his life. Pete the barber also limped.

Like Ethan, he greeted Ordway as though he'd been gone fifteen minutes instead of almost sixteen months. 'Who kicked you in the face?' he snorted as though secretly pleased.

'Pete, I'm going to Mike's office before seeing Bob Koonce in the courthouse,' Channon Ordway answered in kind. 'Bring some tools and a few leeches. Hurry!'

'Why?' asked the barber with infuriating slowness.

'Because the law's breathing a lot closer down my neck than it ever did yourn, you old reprobate,' Ordway managed to grin.

'Law? You mean Step? Bah!' he sneered at the open doorway and the back of a blue bolero jacket moving up the new boardwalk toward Mike's two-story bank.

Despite the brief ladling of personal levity, Channon Ordway's world was as grim and as black as his growth of whiskers. He had written Kathy Perry weeks ago, swearing her to secrecy, informing her that he was very much alive and on his way home with a big herd. A man of twenty-seven returning to the range where he had been born, back to a snub-nosed girl who had loved him very much.

He still couldn't think of her as being married to a lout like Step, but the fact that she had told her husband everything contained in the letter had been the match that blew Channon Ordway's world apart within a matter of hours.

## CHAPTER SIX

Mike Adkins' modest bank faced the new courthouse across the breadth of the street lying like a curved raw scar in the sun. The judicial center for several pioneer counties was still sixty miles away. Only the offices of Sheriff and Justice of the Peace were as yet occupied.

The lower floor and walls of the bank

were of native stone, the upper floor being of hand-sawed planking. Ordway went inside and nodded to a startled teller. The man occupied the same little grilled window where unfortunate Kathy Perry once had worked to earn money for a wedding dress Channon now would never see. She'd worn it the day she married Step Eaton.

Ordway took the stairs along the south wall and emerged into Mike's huge expanse of office on the upper floor. The banker stood before a large plate glass window with a pair of imported Dutch binoculars glued to his eyes. He was looking out over the old part of town toward the promontory's south tip.

'Just watching Sonny and our respected sheriff and their gang of Wyoming cutthroats come up the valley,' he announced pleasantly, turning. 'They're on the road below the rim now.'

'Minus one. Red Waldo. He won't be along.'

'You young ingrate. That's going to cost me a three dollar and eighty cent checking account.' He produced a bottle and glasses. 'How'd you get the eye?'

Ordway told him how, plus the rest of it.

Mike whistled. 'Eric must have been desperate to have bought off your crew. Incidentally, it took the last of his money. You real sure?'

'He paid off my trail crew *double*,' Ordway growled. 'Well, he took his gamble and now he's going to lose.'

'He carries a lot of respect from people who had to stand by while Ethan and Sonny rustled him clean, Chann. But nobody dared to lift a hand or open their mouths. They're the same people who want him for our first judge when this county really gets organized.'

Pete limped in carrying a pail of hot water, towels, and a box containing shears, razor and comb.

'Over here by the big window, Pete,' Ordway said and pulled up a chair. He sat down. 'Do what you can before Sonny and Step get here to take some new orders from Ethan.'

Pete yanked the apron around Ordway's neck and sneered. 'It's allus hurry it up among you damned cow wrastlers. You go a month without a hair cut an' then want it in two minutes. Yer paw an' Ethan was the same way when the law was after us.'

The rapid snip of the shears began and

drowned out Pete's growls. Ordway said, 'Mike, what happened when Step got back here with the herd from Mexico and reported me dead?'

Mike handed him the drink and the apron moved as Ordway's hand reached out and took the glass.

'Hold still!' snarled Pete. 'How in the blue blazes can I . . . ah, go ahead an' drink it!'

Mike said, 'Most of them, including Kathy, believed Step's yarn that you were killed in a revolution down there. Personally, I couldn't see you giving up Kathy, turning native with some girl, and the rest of it.'

Ordway elaborated on what had taken place at the herd and, later, at Randolph's Rocking R ranch. 'How do I stand legally on the ranch and the money Ethan got for the herd in Cheyenne, Mike?' he asked.

'Ethan paid off the fifteen thousand loan and banked nearly thirty more profits here in his own name, Chann. He cooked up some papers, including your will, giving him all the ranch. Wasn't a thing I could do except keep my opinions to myself.'

In a remarkably short time Ordway was trimmed and shaved. Pete pulled the last of the blood heavy leeches from beneath the puffed eyes and drowned them in the bucket of soiled water.

'All right,' he growled to cover his feelings. 'Now go let Sonny close the other one.'

He stalked out and Mike grinned. 'Don't let the old fraud fool you, Chann.' He pointed to his old saddle gun in a scabbard tied to the chair back of his desk. 'He's got his down there in the barber shop, too, Chann.'

'He thinks like he walks, Mike.'

'Him and Hanse and Henry Cartwright and me have talked quite a bit over our Thursday night poker games the past year. We know Ethan is responsible for the death of Eric's brother. We're pretty sure the same goes for old Tobe Whitehouse taking a bullet in the back. We figure Ethan has got to be stopped.'

'Then why didn't you?' asked Ordway shortly.

'Sonny and his gunnies, Chann. They're young and tough like we were in the old days. We've grown old, Chann. We're liquor-sick like Lon Perry, or crippled like Pete. Can you imagine spraddle-footed old Hanse shooting from the back of a running horse? Hell, he weighs in at two hundred seventy.'

'Then why the gun there?'

'We figure that sooner or later Ethan will want the rest of the money in this bank and send Sonny's masked men after it,' Mike Adkins answered softly. 'Call us any damn thing you like, but we still know how to shoot.'

Ordway started for the stairway door. Knob in hand, he turned at the sound of Mike's voice. 'Where you going now?'

'To see Bob Koonce in the courthouse, Mike. I want some more answers.'

'Such as?'

'I want to know why Tobe's adopted son is still wearing a deputy's badge,' was the short reply.

He reached the street level and paused on the bank's porch, looking along the curve towards Pete's shop and the former back door of Hanse's place. Nobody was in sight.

But a chestnut gelding with four white hocks stood tied over in front of the courthouse with Ordway's saddle on and, on the two-step stoop was the figure of a man the same age as Ordway. Koonce stood with a sawed-off Greener dangling in one hand.

His face expressed nothing as Ordway crossed toward him. His brows were like two thick, black worms and there was tremendous power in medium-width shoulders and hands more suited to a much bigger man. Ordway started to speak, scowlingly, but the deputy beat him to it.

'Save it,' he said shortly. 'There's someone inside. I'll wait here.'

Ordway went up the steps and entered a hallway. At the first door to the left he turned the knob. He heard a rustle of organdie and turned. Kathy stood in the doorway leading from the sheriff's inner office.

He was appalled at the change in this once wholesome young girl. Her eyes were two overly bright spots in round dark skin of unnatural and unhealthy hue. She was thin and her hands were twisting nervously. And the protruding round ball at the waist of her dress told its own mute story.

Poor kid! he thought pityingly. She spent her entire life being young mother to a whole brood of little Perrys and now this, all because she believed a scoundrel after I took a couple of bullets in the back.

'Hello, Kathy,' Ordway smiled and went forward with hand outstretched. Anything to put her more at ease. 'I heard over town that you'd married.'

'I knew they'd be quick enough to tell you.'

'I guess things just didn't work out for us, eh?'

'There ain't no use in us crying about it now, Chann,' she said and fought down a moist sniff, her eyes suspiciously damp. 'What's done is done. But I had to see you.'

'What is it, Kathy?'

'There's a couple things I got to ask you.'

Here it comes, he thought with dread. And what was he supposed to tell her? The truth? Try to lie?

'Did Step shoot you in the back down there in Mexico like I heard a few minutes ago?' she asked.

He sought for words, some way of cushioning the harsh, the brutal truth. He found none.

'Somebody did, Kathy,' he answered her gently. 'I didn't actually see him.'

'But he was with you, ridin' right behind you, wasn't he?' she persisted like a child without guile.

'I'm afraid he was, Kathy, and I'm sorry

for your sake.'

'Well,' she said, and a long tired sigh came out of her. 'I guess I must have knowed it was something like that all along.' She gave him a direct look that was completely disconcerting. 'You're going to kill my husband, ain't you, Chann?'

'I'm going to protect myself, Kathy. And I think it best if you go now. He's due in any minute.'

She nodded and left. In the doorway she turned. 'I guess you noticed I'm about ready to have a baby, Chann. I just want you to know I never loved Step deep down. But he had money from Ethan's cattle and I'd have done most anything to get away from Pa's drinkin' and into a clean home of my own.'

'I understand.' Poor kid. You poor unhappy kid. By what destiny, by whose order, did it have to happen to you?

She said: 'I knowed you would. But if you kill Step, mean as he is, I'll have to take my baby back home to Pa.'

Ordway rejoined Koonce just outside the double-door entrance to the courthouse. The deputy didn't look up. He stared across the street at the unsightly rear of the old buildings and the new porches nailed to

85

most of them.

Ordway said dryly, 'Now that you've done your good deed, I've a couple of reasonably good questions to ask—*if* you don't mind, deputy?'

'I'll answer one of them now. I'm still wearing this badge old Tobe pinned on me when I was seventeen because I figger I'm about as close to his killer as I can get.'

'Step?'

'He's been trying for weeks to get up nerve enough to fire me. What was that other question, Chann?' Some of the ice had gone out of him and from Ordway too, something of what had been flowing in. For almost a year the deputy had been blaming Ordway for Kathy Perry's misfortune.

'If I hadn't got loose this morning Step would have finished me off. Didn't you know that, amigo?'

Koonce nodded, his eyes still straight ahead. 'Enough that I followed along until you were in the clear. Couldn't be seen riding back with you, Chann. Might have given Step the nerve to fire me.'

'Then I'll smooth my hackles down, too, Bob,' Channon Ordway said. 'Look—over the top of Hanse's place. There they come.'

The little cavalcade of about a dozen men had lipped up out of Squaw Valley, and for the two men who led it the ride had been anything but pleasant. There had been accusations over Waldo's death, Ordway's escape, and by the time they hove in sight of the old fort they were openly quarrelling.

They pulled up in front of Hanse's low, flat, log edifice grayed by thirty-odd winters.

'Damn, but I need a drink,' Step growled to change the subject and because the thought was uppermost in his mind. 'A real whackin' thirst.'

'Likely runs in the family,' Sonny sneered maliciously. 'Probably caught it from your father-in-law.'

Step made no reply. There was a sullen cast to his liquor-florid features as he stepped upon the awningless porch. Sonny had been that way at every opportunity all the way up the valley from Randolph's ranch.

One corner of the sheriff's mouth held a small cut, still biting from Channon Ordway's smashing blow. Lordy, what was Ethan going to say about this second blooper?

Step almost shuddered as they grouped there on the porch. They were watching a familiar rig drawn by a mare at a sizzling pace whip into view around a building's ax-shaped corner.

'It's the damnedest thing I've ever seen,' Sonny remarked with a grin. 'I've seen old Doc Cartwright make that corner a thousand times in a cloud of dust. Never hit it with a wheel hub yet, never missed it more than six inches.'

'Wonder what it is this time?' somebody asked.

They waited.

Step nervously licked his dry lips. Maybe, just maybe, Ethan had wounded Chann. No, he decided. Ethan didn't wound, he killed swiftly with a terrible black vengeance. Could be it was the other way around. Chann was too much like his father Tim.

Henry Cartwright pulled the panting mare up close by the edge of Hansen's porch and jumped down like a gray-goateed bantam rooster off its morning perch. He reached in by the seat, brought forth a kettle-shaped iron anchor with a rope already tied to the sorrel mare's neck, and placed it on the ground as though the mare needed visual proof right under his nose not to stray.

Big black bag in hand, he stepped upon the porch toward the assembled toughs of Sonny's gang.

'Get your damned thieves out of my way, Sonny,' he greeted another of the sons of old outlaw friends he'd delivered.

Sonny spoke without rancor. 'You seem to be in a mite of a hurry, Doc.'

Cartwright ignored him until he reached the doors in the old log structure. 'So were you the night I hauled you out of your mammy while your paw lay cut to pieces after a drunken knife fight,' he snapped.

'Doc,' Step asked, licking at his dry lips, 'who all's hurt in there?'

'Ethan. But he's probably got enough venom left so's you won't get off scot-free for letting a prisoner escape.'

'Shooting?'

'No, worse luck, Chann's got too much of his mother and father in him. He just worked Ethan over with a gun barrel. Now stay the hell out of that back room while I'm working, understand?'

'He sure means it too,' chuckled Sonny at the emptily swinging doors. 'Even back in the old days, that scrappy little cuss never took no stink off any badman he ever had to work on.'

They walked over to the west wall bar as Cartwright opened a rear room door and disappeared after closing it. At the bar Hansen, with no word of greeting except a hard scowl, began to set up bottles and glasses. He was hoping that Step wouldn't treat and try to sign another chit.

After today Step Eaton's credit was a thing of the past in here. So was his presence.

The sheriff poured a generous splash into a glass and downed it. He glanced at the closed door back there and wondered what was going on. Through a window he saw that a west wind had pursed its lips and blown puffballs into the distant sky. They hung up there around the crags below the snowy peaks like smoke rings.

At this moment the sheriff of Tulac was afraid. More afraid than he'd ever been in his life. 'Hanse, give me a pencil. How bad is Ethan hurt?'

Hanse said with cold imperturbability: 'No backshooter signs a chit in this place or comes in anymore. Your bar bill is cancelled. Now that Chann is back you ain't goin' to live long enough to pay me anyhow. Finish your drink and get out, Step.'

'Well, now,' Sonny breathed the words softly at the giant. 'What have we got in Tulac all of a sudden?'

'I don't owe you anything either,' Hanse rumbled ominously. 'I paid it all the night we took your father out of the hands of some vigilantes up in Alder Gulch, Montana.'

One monster hand lay under the bar and Sonny knew that it contained a .45, that the muzzle was pointed right at his belly, and that the tough old owl hooter would kill him with one shot if he made another wrong move.

'All right, Hanse,' Sonny Shackleford replied meekly.

It was a gift he'd acquired a long time ago, being meek at the right time. It had worked with Eric Randolph today, too.


## CHAPTER SEVEN

Inside the back room, Doc Cartwright had placed the big bag on the green-topped

91

table near where Ethan Ordway's thick forearms were crossed. The shaggy black head rested face down between them. Below it was a fresh pool of blood.

Now Ethan lifted his lion's mane of hair and flung it back, and Cartwright saw that poetic justice had been done: one of Ethan's eyes also was closed. Deliberately, the little man suspected.

'Don't talk,' he snapped. 'I've got eyes!'

He slid out of his coat and rolled up white shirt sleeves. After pouring alcohol on his hands to disinfect, he pushed Ethan's head back and sat it at a proper angle on the neck, like a barber ready to apply comb and scissors. He parted the bruised lips and ran fingers inside.

'One knocked out and two more broken off, Ethan,' he pronounced. 'I can pry out the stumps, of course, but if you've got any sense you'll start for Denver in a fast buggy with Sonny driving.'

Ethan caught the import and made his answer. His decision to kill Chann Ordway had already been irrevocably posted. No side-track traveling!

'Get them out and hurry,' he slobbered thickly. 'I've got work to do, Henry.'

'I know what it is!'

'Then don't try anything funny, such as drugging me. If you do I'll kill you.'

Cartwright fixed him with piercing, antagonistic eyes. 'Don't you ever, don't you *ever*, threaten me like that again or I'll shotgun you, Ethan.'

He brought out a bottle containing some pills, administered them to kill pain, and went to work. Fifteen minutes later the job was crudely but efficiently finished, the bleeding stopped. Ethan, his barrel-battered features salved but not bandaged, could talk with a thickened slur.

Doc pulled off the last of three leeches beneath the eye and stepped back. 'There,' he said with strange quietness, 'now go start your blood bath, the rape and pillage of what has become a decent country. Forget everything decent you might have become and revert to what we all were thirty years ago. Then take your place in hell with Shackleford, your brother Tim, with old Koonce and Tobe Whitehouse and the others. Wait there a few years and we'll *all* have a big reunion!'

He rolled down his sleeves, buttoned them at the wrists, snapped the bag shut with a vicious metallic sound, and put on his coat.

'Go tell Step to come in here,' Ethan commanded.

Cartwright caught the tossed gold eagle and picked up his bag. 'When a man chases the devil around the stump as long as you have, my friend, he finds out too late that he's finally caught up with it.'

He closed the door and walked toward the bar. Ignoring the questions in a dozen or more pairs of eyes, he placed the coin upon the bar and indicated the crowd.

'Disinfect it, Hanse, before you serve the house. I don't want it.

Doctor Henry Cartwright, M.D., Physician and Surgeon, turned and bent a baleful stare upon Step Eaton, Sheriff. He jerked his thumb in the direction from which he had just come.

'Go on back there and pull down your drawers,' he sneered at the flush-faced lawman. 'Teacher is waiting with a switch.'

He spat disgustedly and left the low-ceilinged saloon to its own thoughtful silence. The symptoms showed an epidemic about to erupt in Tulac. Probable cure, and an old reliable one: gunfire.

He replaced the kettle-shaped anchor, got into the buggy, pulled the mare around and sent her at a sizzling trot toward the ax-squared corner of an old log building. A hard jar, and Cartwright was almost flung out of the buggy as the left rear wheel bounced off the building's corner.

'Well, I'll be bedoodled,' Cartwright muttered disgustedly as he looked back. 'Henry, Mike Adkins was right. You *are* getting old!'

★　　　★　　　★

At the rear room door Step Eaton squared his shoulders in an effort to pump another inch of height and a pound or two of whiskey courage before facing Ethan. He would have felt less trepidation had he known the room contained a half-dozen rattlesnakes.

Sonny, loaded with the kind of cash these days that Step formerly possessed, had jeeringly bought several rounds, jeered as Step drank them, knowing how much the sheriff needed false courage. Well, Step told himself, maybe cocky Sonny was wrong. Maybe the time was at hand to show a few people that Eaton had guts. Sure, right now! Step boldly decided.

He'd face Ethan, listen to his roar, then go straight to the courthouse and fire that black-browed deputy whose brooding eyes always seemed to be fixed at a point between the sheriff's shoulder blades.

Step could feel them each time he turned his back on old Tobe's adopted son. Koonce was playing a waiting game, wearing him down a glance at a time, waiting for evidence of murder. Well, let 'em prove it first!

That first time had been a tough one, putting two slugs into Chann Ordway's back. But, once the ice was broken, the second time was much easier—and thorough too. Old Tobe never knew what hit him.

'And there'll be a third time too, by God, 'less'n somebody watches their step,' Eaton growled bravely and shoved open the door.

Ethan sat with a huge hand wrapped around a tumbler of whisky. Light from the window glistened upon his greasy face. 'Close that door!'

The courage drained out of Step. Just those three words and he was dog-whipped again, the way he had been with Ethan all his life, and he knew it.

'If you've got any lies ready, throw them out,' Ethan rumbled ominously. 'I want the truth of what happened down there today.'

He listened in scathing silence until the sheriff finished talking. Nor did Step hold back anything. You didn't hold out on a man like Ethan Ordway.

He watched sardonically as Step picked up the bottle and poured himself a badly needed drink. 'Now that you let him get away, just what do you aim to do about it?' he inquired.

Step tossed off the slug. 'Go after him,' he answered bravely.

'Good. He's right here in town. It ought to be easy.'

'I ain't got a chance against him with a short gun, and you know it, you black devil. Red Waldo's gun was out and levelled when Chann shot him. I got to have time to do it in my own way.'

Ethan rose to his feet. The room automatically became smaller, the ceiling lower. His bulk seemed to compress the air, the very breath in Step Eaton's lungs.

'Now you listen to me, you bottle-slobbering, wife-beating excuse for a man!' Ethan Ordway snarled from back of a levelled finger long and black like a gun barrel, and ten times more dangerous. 'Time has run out for you. It ran out when you let Chann get away from the Randolph spread. Thanks to your stupidity I've not only lost the best brand-blotter I ever saw work, but Sonny and his whole crew will now have to pull out of there.'

'I think what you really want me to do is get killed so's you can give Sonny this badge,' Step growled in a sudden burst of bravado.

'Don't think I haven't considered that possibility since you began the battle of the bottle,' Ethan replied calmly. 'I have.'

'Well, what do you want me to do now?' Step growled sullenly, reaching for the bottle.

'Get rid of Chann. And fast, before people wake up and give him a hand.' Ethan added mercilessly, 'It's your scalp or his, make your choice.'

'Oh, yeah?' Step blustered, desperate, but still amazed at himself. 'Now let me tell you something! A lot of old-timers thought it damn strange that the day three gunmen braced you in this place one of them was Jude Waldo. Then Tim came to your rescue and got killed. A lot of other old-timers thought it damn strange that while you killed *two* of them gunmen, Jude Waldo killed Tim Ordway and escaped to Cheyenne. You never went after him. You never even said nothing to Red about it—'

Ethan's right hand dropped the glass and flashed to the bottle. He slapped it from Eaton's hand and sent it rolling into a corner, where it lay gurgling.

'Get out of here, you ungrateful scum. Get out of here and keep your whiskey mouth shut and kill Chann Ordway before you die,' Ethan hissed, his face a hideous mask.

Step slunk out the back way and onto the makeshift new porch, where the bottles and trash used to be. Ethan stepped to the door leading to the bar, and stuck his head through. 'Sonny, come back here,' he ordered.

Sonny came in as Ethan was picking up the bottle and setting it back on the blood-topped table. 'He's drinking far too much lately, Ethan,' the young tough said, reading the significance and having heard the sound.

'It probably cost you a pardner today.'

'I oughta killed him for it.'

'Why didn't you?'

'Thought maybe you might not like it. He shined your boots the first twelve years and licked them the next twelve.'

Ethan changed the subject. 'So

99

Randolph chased you off the place after hearing a few things, huh?'

Sonny nodded, then shook his head when the big man indicated the bottle and sat down again. He himself took a chair, removed his battered hat and pushed back his tawny hair.

'He did, and I didn't bat an eye either. Not with three rifles staring us in the face, Eric's lined right at my mouth. If I had made one move, opened my big mouth, he'd have shot me dead.'

'Them women, too?'

'Hell,' Sonny said, not without admiration. 'They've hunted animals all their lives, and to them two women that's just what we was. Animals. We packed and got out.'

'Maybe it's better this way. We've got his herd rebranded, but one thing has kept me from coming into the open until now. Ever kill a woman, Sonny?'

'Coupla Ute squaws,' Sonny shrugged indifferently.

'Supposin' their skins are white?'

'If it has to be done.'

'First things first. Chann. He's here in town. Get your men and get right on it, Sonny. I've figgered a way to get legal title

100

to Squaw Valley.'

Sonny rose to his feet and put on his hat. 'What about Step?'

The words came a little cautiously, warily.

'If he gets lucky on a third try, fine. We'll judge him later. If not—' Ethan shrugged.

'We're rid of him and I get his badge,' Sonny Shackleford finished. 'Fair enough, I reckon.'

He happened to glance out the window and then turned. 'I just wish to hell you'd get up and come over here and take a look,' he sneered disgustedly.

\*　　\*　　\*

The object of their conversation, full of both whiskey and new determination to start afresh with the whole world, had lurched off Hansen's new and much cussed porch and out into the street. He'd forgotten his black racing mare, racked out front with a dead man's reins—Waldo's— on the bridle.

Right now Step was obsessed with the determination to carry out his silent threats of several months: fire Bob Koonce and

101

dare him to do something about it!

Mike happened to come by from the bank, curious to see how Ethan looked and to keep abreast of developments. Thankful for any excuse to delay his journey on across the street, the sheriff swerved, lurched over and tried to block his path.

'Where'n the hell do you think you're goin'?' Eaton demanded truculently. He had spotted Kathy's brown-dressed, thick-waisted figure crossing from the court-house toward Ethan's livery, probably to weep on the old drunk's shoulder.

Likely she'd heard the truth about the shooting in Mexico and gone running to her staunch, sympathetic friend, Koonce. Maybe she wanted the deputy to arrest him. Step's alcoholic mind threshed about. So she wanted Chann back now, huh? Nice little frame-up. Her, Chann, and Koonce.

This town needed a clean-up and now was the time to start.

'Answer me!' Step Eaton bawled at the banker.

A look of disgust crossed Mike's face. He never wore a hat except during blizzards. His white hair shone like the tops of those thunderheads floating below timberline like ducks swimming around a tule patch.

'Get out of my way,' Mike said quietly, icicles dripping from every word.

'Hell, I will! How come you think you're so high and mighty you won't loan a few dollars? Where'd you ever get enough money to start a bank with anyhow, hah!' the sheriff shouted.

'Go find another whipping boy, Step,' Mike advised. 'I suppose you'll go home and take it out on your wife. Henry Cartwright says you've become a very good at it lately.'

'I knew it!' Step Eaton, yelled angrily. 'She used to work for you to buy a weddin' dress, and you're in with 'em too. Maybe you slipped her a little extra money along—'

But Mike, his nose wrinkling with loathing for something unclean, had passed him by. The sheriff, unaware of how many eyes were watching him with something of the same in them, turned and pursued his course toward the courthouse once more.

Again he spotted Kathy who, heavy-footed, was trying to walk a little faster. She, along with everybody else along the short street, had overheard. Again the little jab of fear struck through the alcoholic rage and frustration in Step's brain. Again he found excuse not to face his deputy and ask for the badge old Tobe had pinned on a seventeen year old youth ten years before.

Glad of that excuse, Step lurched on in the middle of the curved team-and-scraper scar, toward the corral.

Inside the courthouse two men had been talking. Many things that had formed a silent, distant barrier between them were swept away. They were looking at Step's lurching progress past the horse tied out front with Ordway's flat-horn Mexican saddle strapped on and the Sharp's in its boot.

'Look at the killer,' Koonce said bitterly. 'I know he did it, it would be so easy to knock out this window and cut him down with eighteen buckshot.'

'You'd be doing everybody in town a favor, Kathy included.'

'Except me. I don't have to live with them. Just myself, Chann.'

'What are you going to do, let him beat her up? Her and poor old Lon?'

'No,' Koonce said. 'I can stop that. I can wait just a little while longer.'

Ordway followed him back outside, but as they stepped down the two steps to a boardwalk leading fifty or sixty feet out to the courthouse hitch-rail and a proud pine flag-pole, all of thirty feet high, new movement caught their eyes.

About a dozen heavily armed horsemen came in sight.

Sonny's men had mounted on the old south side of Hansen's place, ridden west a hundred yards to a fifty-yard gap separating a store and Ethan's livery, then swung north into the new street toward the courthouse.

'I guess,' Koonce said, his eyes glinting like polished lead marbles, 'that Step will have to wait.'

'So soon,' Ordway commented dryly. 'Ethan didn't lose any time giving new orders.'

'Ethan never in all his life got gun-whupped neither,' the grim deputy replied. 'Let's get to that Sharps. The range is too great for this Greener.'

They moved along the boardwalk, out and away from the courthouse, toward the saddled horse. The sun was almost down, Ordway was surprised to note. The thunderheads were being henna'd with copper.

Ordway said, 'Maybe we won't have to do the job, Bob.'

Step Eaton had lurched out and thrown up both hands in the universal gesture that

105

meant halt.

He stood belligerently in front of them, fists now jammed upon his hips, elbows akimbo. He wasn't aware of his danger, only of the amused lights in the eyes of Sonny and his mounted toughs.

He bawled the same words at the horsemen that he'd bawled at Mike. 'Where'n the hell do you think you're goin'?'

The amused lights dancing wickedly in Sonny's eyes faded and the dance was over. 'Make just one move and you're dead. I'd do it anyhow but I haven't got a second to spare.'

His eyes forgot Step, were upon two men approaching a freshly saddled horse. On that horse, in a saddle boot, was the deadliest rifle in this country. If Ordway got to it Sonny could die quickly.

He raised himself in his stirrups. 'Chann! Not another step toward that gun. Bob! Go back in that courthouse if you know what's good for you.'

No answer. The two men were within thirty feet of that rifle. And if Ordway got to it Sonny could never get out of range in time. If he got to that horse he'd get away while a shotgun and Koonce's six-shooter were blasting.

A simple solution came to Sonny's mind. A short, explosive laugh broke from Ethan Ordway's protégé. First things first. The horse . . .

Sonny bent and snapped his repeater from its own scabbard. He whipped it to his shoulder with a single fast motion. A hard report rang out. A bullet whacked loudly, distinctly.

A scream broke from the tied horse. It screamed again as another bullet into its lungs sent it crashing down. It lay there futilely, its head held off the ground because of the close tied reins around the rail.

A bright flood of crimson gushed upward and out of its mouth and nostrils as it screamed a strangled death cry.

Echoing it came the sound of Sonny Shackleford's jeering laughter. No matter what happened next, he'd put Ordway afoot.

And the odds now stood at a dozen to two.

It was time for Ethan to come out into the open, to take over and combine Pronghorn Basin and Squaw Valley into the greatest cow outfit in all Colorado and a few other states and territories.

He'd failed once to keep Squaw Valley, where Chann Ordway had been born in a stinking Indian tepee. Now he'd finally figured out how to get around that legal stuff. All that stood in the way were two men.

Two against a dozen tough guns.

## CHAPTER EIGHT

Sonny bent forward and with a deft flick of the wrist choked the lethal short range weapon back into the scabbard under his left leg. He straightened and looked down at the sheriff with a contemptuous sneer. Fifty yards to one side, in the livery corral, Kathy Eaton stood beside her father and watched the scene while a grulla horse on a lead rope drank its fill.

Sonny had time now. The dead horse had fallen on Ordway's rifle and pinned it under several hundred pounds of weight. Or so it appeared from here.

'Now you look here—' Eaton began to bluster.

'Oh, shut up, booze head,' Sonny flung

down at him. 'Go on home and sleep it off.'

He glanced around at his men. 'All right, boys. Easy now and spread out.'

Two or three of the men looked doubtful, but none hesitated. They moved forward at a slow walk. Sonny was banking that those two men he'd been raised with would not open fire first. By then it would be too late.

'Hey, Bob,' he called to the deputy, hand dangling close to his right hip, reins lifted. 'You got a last chance. Get back in that courthouse or take what's coming.'

Koonce didn't reply. The two men waited. They were within six feet of the dead horse when suddenly Channon Ordway sprang. Before Sonny realized what had happened the Sharps was out of the scabbard and Ordway lay with it levelled over the saddle.

'Keep coming!' Ordway called piercingly to Sonny. 'And the first man who moves makes you dead.'

Sonny had cockily, overconfidently walked himself into a death trap. He turned sick inside when he saw the double-barrel go up and knew that he was done for.

'Hey, Step!' he called back over his shoulder. 'Come over here and call off your watchdog before somebody gets killed.'

'Put down that shotgun, you hear?' Step bawled, more in fear of Ethan than a desire to keep Sonny alive. He'd taken everything off the young tough today: sneers, jeers, insults. And there could be no doubt that Sonny wanted old Tobe Whitehouse's badge.

Koonce, however, ignored the sheriff. The ominous Greener was swinging back and forth, and every man swept by the muzzles knew that if he made a move to draw a gun he would be the first to die. Ordway also was up on his feet, his Sharps covering Sonny.

And Sonny had seen what the big cartridge weapon could do to a man. Close up. Today.

Step came puffing up, his face beef-red from liquor and running. He stopped and spread his legs like a played out horse. No matter what happened this was the opportunity, the one chance he'd been hoping for to hurdle the problem that had confronted him since four obsequious county commissioners under Ethan's orders had made him sheriff.

'You're fired!' he shouted, levelling a finger at the deputy.

'All right, I'm fired,' Koonce replied. 'Sonny, get down off that horse or you're dead.'

'Ethan!' cried out Sonny, his voice edged with panic. Never in his brutal, cow-thief years had he ever found himself in a situation such as this. And, as in past years since his father had been hanged, he was calling upon his mentor to get him out.

'Ethan!' he called again like a child to its father.

Channon Ordway shifted his glance and the muzzle of the Sharps toward Hansen's bastard back porch, now his front porch, and the men there. Ethan's battered face stood out clear over the front sight.

'Sheriff,' Ethan's voice came in the eerie silence. 'Turn that prisoner loose. Sonny, ride out.'

'Sonny stays until I go, Ethan,' Ordway called. He twisted his neck and looked at Koonce. 'Can you keep them until I get clear of town? If it's going to be fox and hounds I want a start.'

'They'll keep.'

'How about you?'

'I took care of myself for ten years behind this badge. I still can now that I won't be wearing it anymore.'

111

He spoke to the sheriff as he unpinned the pentacle. 'I kept this badge clean for all those years. But as long as you've dirtied it that's where you'll pick it up.'

It cleaved the air and fell at the sheriff's feet. The sun was gone and a chill was in the air. Like the day was ending, something else was ending as a sheriff's office star lay in the street near the carcass of a dead horse.

Sonny Shackleford laughed as he reined his horse around and, his arrogance restored, waved for his men to follow. He knew he wouldn't be shot in the back and the knowledge brought forth a hidden sneer. It damn well would have been different had the harness been on the other end of the horse!

Koonce said to Step Eaton: 'I know in my heart that you killed old Tobe. Even if you didn't, you still deserve killin' for what you are, what you did to Chann and Kathy. You are finished, Step.'

'Now, look here—'

'Bob, cover my back while I make a run through Hanse's saloon. I'll take that black mare. If Step makes a move kill him for me.'

Ordway broke into a trot across the

street, an odd figure in *vaquero* clothing and big hat. The peso rowels of a dead Mexican general rattled at last. He carried the Sharps in his left hand, his six-shooter in his right.

His eyes bored into those of Ethan as he came close. 'Hanse, take Ethan's gun until I get through. I've already taken two bullets in the back because of this mad scoundrel. Give me two minutes.'

'You've got them,' Hansen replied. 'If it wasn't for Sonny and his outfit coming after me I'd finish him right here.'

Ordway entered the darkened interior of the saloon and darted across a dance floor unused for twenty years except on special occasions. The black mare flared her nostrils as he untied Red Waldo's reins. He went into leather and not a moment too soon. From a point two hundred yards away, to the west, Sonny Shackleford and his men emerged into view in the broken teeth gap near Ethan's livery.

A yell went up and a rifle spanged.

The game of fox and hounds had begun.

Ordway dug in the rowels and felt the tremendous surge of silk-smooth muscles. Seventy-five yards away was timber and through it the road leading down into

Pronghorn Basin. Ordway and the fast running mare disappeared into it.

The entire crowd who had been on the north porch of the saloon now came boiling out of the old south end, funneling through like a herd milling at a corral gate. Ethan Ordway's giant figure knocked men aside like tenpins as he plunged toward his own horse.

His own horse, like the black mare, had been beaten about the head, and Ethan's dive for the reins startled the frightened animal. Ethan lost a couple of minutes, holding onto the reins and cursing the frightened, circle-plunging animal, before he finally got mounted. A grunt went out of the beast as his great knees slammed into its ribs and then rowel steel bit into its sides.

He swept down the road in the wake of his hoodlum pack, and one of the silent men who watched him go was Mike Adkins. His was the only grin among them. 'I was waiting for Step to get liquor-broke enough to mortgage that mare to me for a loan. I could take her to Denver and Cheyenne and country-boy clean up those gambling city slickers.'

'You gone crazy?' Hansen snorted disgustedly. 'She's been outrun by every

114

crow bait, ewe-necked, hammer-head Indian pony in this country.'

'She's been *out-sprinted*,' Mike said wickedly. 'I know her background, and there's no horse in Colorado who can catch her on a fifty mile run.'

'She's a high-strung bitch who can rear and break more bridle reins than any horse I ever saw. Hell, she'll even chew a knot loose. If she was mine I'd give her to the Utes for a feast.'

Henry Cartwright joined them, three men from the old days, and a fourth appeared at a run. Lon Perry's face was streaming blood.

'Henry.' He was sobbing like a child. 'Come quick to the corral.'

'What's the matter, Lon?'

'It's Kathy!' the handyman gasped, tears streaming from his eyes. 'Step knocked me down first and then started beating her. She's layin' over there by the water trough. And, Henry, there's blood coming from under her skirts.'

'That goddamned son-of-a-bitch!' Doc Cartwright swore savagely. 'If she dies, I'll kill him!'

'He's gone!' sobbed Perry. 'Grabbed a saddle horse and lit hard for his house.'

'Where's Koonce?'

'After him. But afoot.'

★    ★    ★

Channon Ordway rode out of the timber and, in the dusk, saw far away and below him the familiar panorama of Pronghorn Basin. In the dying light a wagon road lay there like a piece of tossed string.

Five miles away, directly in the center of the huge grassy bowl, was an old, weatherbeaten dot. He knew every yard of the basin, every foot of the road, every inch of that house.

He had been born within a few miles of it all.

He turned in the saddle and looked back. But his pursuers either were afraid of a deadly ambush or were waiting for Ethan and darkness. Well, neither would be long in coming.

They could afford their time, guessing correctly Ordway's probable destination; figuring he might fort-up and try to reduce their dozen men by several.

It was full night by the time Ordway covered the five miles. He rode past familiar corrals and sheds, all now deserted because Ethan spent only the nights here when the mood suited him. There were no cattle in the basin, although Ethan probably had some plans to change *that* in the very near future.

Ordway rode directly to the kitchen porch with its roofed over well-sweep above the ancient cistern. The odor of sour trash came to his nose as he swung down. God alone only knew what had been tossed from the porch by rough uncouth men like Sonny and the others, now somewhere out there in the night. It came to Ordway with something of a shock that the place looked smaller than in former years. Older. Against the night sky the kitchen stovepipe tilted precariously in the arms of loose guy wires.

Ordway stumbled and almost fell into more trash as he dismounted. Grunting an execration at Ethan, he crossed the porch to the kitchen door and reached a hand to open it. Then he froze.

Was it his imagination or had he heard a board creek inside. Was it the weather popping ancient flooring? Or had somebody heard him coming and shifted weight?

With Colt ready he leaned back a trifle

and crashed the door open with single drive of his Mexican boot and leaped aside.

'Don't move, Mr. Ordway, or you are dead!' came Eric Randolph's voice. It was grim, icy.

'In all my gray-whiskered years,' Ordway said exasperatedly, 'I have never seen a man as determined to get himself killed as you are, Randolph.'

'Wait!' Vernell's voice cried out. 'We've made a mistake. We thought you were Ethan Ordway.'

A match flared in her hands as he came in. It outlined the faces of Mrs. Randolph and the one of her grimly determined husband. Ordway bowed and spoke sardonically. *Mi casa es su casa.* As we Mexicans say, "My house is your house."'

'Please,' the girl said. 'Don't mock us. We came here tonight on a terrible errand and right now I'm trembling with relief.'

'What errand, may I ask?'

Randolph said quietly: 'We held a family conference today after driving Sonny and his men from the ranch. It's a part of family tradition, when big decisions are to be made. We came to the unhappy conclusion that within a few hours you would be dead, that in order to survive, Ethan Ordway had to die.'

'And you decided to hide out here until he came.'

'I almost shot you before you could speak, Mr. Ordway.'

The match went out and a wave of darkness engulfed the four of them. Ordway, sheathing his Colt, said: 'If you belonged in this country you would have. That's why I think you should get out of it now while you're all still alive.'

'And let you fight your uncle to see which of you gets Bitter Squaw?' Vernell's voice flashed with sudden, desperate bitterness. 'You'd like that, wouldn't you, Mr. Ordway?'

He ignored the thrust and lit a lamp. In its glow he saw a filthy table piled with dirty dishes, saucers filled with cigarette butts, blackened pans filled with more soured food.

A big rat ran across the cold stove, thudded to the floor, and scurried behind the wood box.

An overwhelming feeling of disgust came over Ordway. There was a sickness in it, a bitter nostalgia for a home once scrubbed clean as only a proud, beautiful woman could scrub it.

Looking at the littered table, Ordway remembered with anger how his mother had placed napkins there which Ethan, scowlingly bent over his plate, ignored.

There was a two-gallon can of kerosene back of the stove. Ordway removed the raw potato universally used throughout the ranching country in lieu of a screw cap cover. He happened to glance up and saw three pairs of eyes watching him, in Vernell's a strange wonder.

'This was my home,' he said bitterly. 'This was the kitchen from which my mother fled into a snowstorm a few hours before I was born.'

He picked up the lamp and flung it hard against the wall as a gasp came from the two women. Fire leaped up and began to eat hungrily at peeling wall paper put there by his mother's own hands. In its light three people, a man and his wife and his niece, saw a face they would never forget. An almost swarthy, terrible face.

In that face was the same terrible thing Vernell had seen as he stood with a hot six-shooter in his hand and fired a third shot into Red Waldo's toad-shaped body sagging against the porch support in Squaw Valley.

Ordway thought: *I know now that I could never have lived here with Kathy. There would have been too many memories, too many reminders of the yesterdays and—*

He didn't realize that he spoke the rest of it aloud. 'And for me there are no yesterdays.'

'I beg your pardon,' Randolph said politely.

'Thinking out loud. Randolph, I respect the determination that brought you here, I admire it even though a decision born of desperation. But Ethan Ordway is out in the open now as leader of Sonny's gang of range toughs.'

'What are you suggesting?'

'That your women are no safer than you are. Take them and get out.'

He spoke directly to Mrs. Randolph. If he was aware that her grave eyes were searching his face, searching for what lay back of its grim mask, he gave no sign.

'Three times today I've displayed weakness. I was grateful to you for kindness. I couldn't stain your home with a coward's blood. And I disfigured my uncle's face into bloody pulp with a gun barrel instead of killing him.'

'You did that?' she murmured.

'Get your people out of here fast and to Koonce in town. Stay there until this thing is settled one way or another. We've got company coming.'

He walked from the kitchen and its crackling flames. He went through a parlor and into another room. The ancient flooring creaked. When he sloshed Kerosene and lit it and stepped back, he realized suddenly how big a room could be in childhood, how small it is twenty-seven years later.

Small and crudely built and so very, very old. Unaware that Vernell had followed him he stood looking at books by the hundreds in floor-to-ceiling shelves. Musty and with gaps in them like broken teeth. Ethan, who had installed his bed in here after Ordway left on his presumed fatal trip to Mexico, had used them for winter fuel in a corner stove.

'Memories?' came the girl's gentle voice in sympathy.

'Too many,' he grunted at her as flames crackled louder. 'I was educated in this room while my mother lived. I lived in it for fifteen years after her death, and only the books kept Ethan from turning me into another Sonny Shackleford or Step Eaton.'

He unscrewed the main cap off the top of the can and she watched with growing sickness of heart as he splashed streams of the incendiary liquid over books and shelves. He soaked the rumpled bed and Ethan's filthy, odorous blankets.

The room became an inferno as he backed away, driven by the heat. 'Get out of here!' he shouted above the increasing roar.

'You'd better hurry, too, Mr. Ordway,' Mrs. Randolph called. 'Eric heard your horse rear and caught it. Riders are coming very fast.'

A trail of fire followed him from room to room until they came to a final door at the east porch, where outside Randolph held the nervous horses. Poor unfortunate Kathy, he thought bitterly. She had planned so much to paint here and fix there. Now it was all over and done with. He felt nothing except a strange sense of relief.

Something vile had been drawn out of him like pus out of a festering sore. He felt clean again.

It was in the past and no man could ever go back and pick up that past.

Ordway flung the empty can from him

and followed the two women. He didn't look back. The high-strung mare, afraid of a fist blow, tried to rear and he brought her down with an iron hand and went up into leather.

The Randolphs broke free and spurred away, expecting that he would follow. Channon Ordway watched them go and rode away as a group of hard running riders, led by an insanely screaming madman, pounded toward the burning ranch house.

## CHAPTER NINE

Out in the basin Channon Ordway pulled up and sat there for a few moments for a final glimpse of home. Flames were leaping like dragons' tongues from all windows. Ordway wasn't certain but he thought he heard some fool begin to fire his pistol.

The black mare moved on into the night at a fast trot. A half mile south of the burning ranch house a low mound, round like a grassy blister on the face of the basin floor, loomed up. In the night he saw the fence of white picket and the headstones.

He had come to say good-bye, possibly a final one.

But he heard horses coming almost at him, loping through the lush spring grass, and he grabbed the Sharps off the saddle. However, his trained ears told him the number. Three.

'Over here,' he called piercingly.

A man couldn't even say good-bye to his family without the presence of these three.

They came up the slope and saw the little fenced plot with five graves and then they were silent. Eric Randolph finally spoke up. 'Really. I'm afraid we've intruded again. Please accept our apologies, Mr. Ordway.'

'We didn't know,' Mrs. Randolph added. 'We have never before been in the basin, you know.'

'It's all right,' Ordway replied. 'The two big stones belong to my father and mother. He was killed in a shoot-out, trying to save Ethan's life, and she never got over it.'

'How tragic. And the others?'

'Two stillborns and a small sister who toddled out into a corral full of green bronks one day.'

He put on his hat and reined over. In the distance the flames made a pillar of fire in

125

the night. Within an hour old Pronghorn Ranch would be but a heaping pile of exploding coals.

'I can still hardly believe it,' Eric Randolph spoke as the four of them rode in silence across the basin toward Tulac. 'A man burning his own home.'

'Lucky for you,' Ordway said almost shortly. 'God only knows what might have happened to you.'

In the night a bright spot appeared unseen in the girl's cheeks. Sonny had been pretty blunt and coarse with her during their last minutes on the Rocking R. Had she told Eric he would have shot the tough dead.

They came at last to where the wagon road climbed up the west side of the basin and into Tulac. Here and there in the night stood little groups of people still watching the fire.

Impelled by some impulse she wasn't sure of, Vernell spoke to Ordway. 'Well,' she inquired, 'on the assumption that you don't break your word, Mr. Ordway, when will the Rocking R in Bitter Squaw be next?'

'Come on,' he growled. 'We've got to find Koonce.'

He turned for a final look east. Far out there in the basin was a mass of glowing coals, a cigarette butt in the basin's night-clenched lips.

'I'm sorry,' she said. 'Any regrets?'

'No,' Channon Ordway said. 'My only regret was that I was too soft and let my uncle live instead of killing him this afternoon.'

'Soft?' she repeated and turned wide eyes upon her aunt. Under her breath she whispered. 'Soft? God in heaven!'

They came to Hanse's deserted place. A curious face stuck itself out over the swing doors and then Mike Adkins came fully into view. His glance took in the four riders sitting in the overflow of light from within.

'I didn't think they'd catch that black mare because I know the man who bred her. So you burned Ethan out, huh? Good!'

'The admirable fellow did it to pull my family and myself out of what could have been a fatal spot,' the easterner replied.

'No,' Ordway said. 'That's why I rode out there.'

'Where you going now?' Mike wanted to know.

'To put these people under Koonce's protection if they've got sense enough to stay there.'

Mike stepped off the porch and came closer and looked up. 'Henry Cartwright is with him. They're at Step's house. Step hurt her with his fists and her baby came. Prematurely. Stillborn.'

'Where's Step now?'

'He grabbed a horse and went home in a cloud of dust. He was out with his rifle and some food by the time Bob got there with the shotgun to kill him. He's out there somewhere tonight with a long range rifle, he's shocked sober, and he probably won't come back again until somebody is dead.'

'I see. Mike, Doc Cartwright once told me privately that Ethan likely was mildly insane. Chances are that the gun beating and ranch burning has tipped him over the edge. Watch your step . . . and your bank!'

He gigged the black mare into motion and the three silent easterners followed.

One of the prices Step Eaton had been willing to pay in order to get Kathy Perry was a neat home of white and yellow native stone on the west side of town. At the front fence were several horses and a couple of vehicles. Neighbors came in time of need. They stood about in hushed little groups.

Near Doc Cartwright's buggy Ordway

dismounted from the black mare, careful to avoid the square of light splashing out through the front door into Kathy's carefully prepared spring flower beds. Step might just be lurking around with his Winchester.

Ordway made no effort to help the two women dismount. They rode horses like they handled a sporting rifle: capably. As Ordway once had heard the story, Eric Randolph had spent years in India as a top governmental administrator.

'It's a lovely little place,' Mrs. Randolph remarked, removing her riding gloves as the four of them went up the walk between the flower beds. Ordway kept in the dark as much as possible.

'You always seem to say the right thing,' Ordway said with a wintry smile. 'That makes it a bit more difficult to dislike the other members of the family.'

Koonce came to the front door, Greener in one hand. Apparently he also thought Step might be around. Beyond his outlined figure, in the kitchen, an elderly woman was almost up to her elbows in a pan of dough. Tobe Whitehouse's widow, Koonce's stepmother.

When tragedy struck at a small town

family, no members cooked. By an unwritten law, that was a duty of neighbors and friends. By this time tomorrow night there would be cakes and pies from as far as ten miles away.

'How's Kathy, Bob?' Ordway inquired of the now ex-deputy.

'Doc Cartwright thinks she might make it, poor kid. I hear there was quite a bonfire out in the basin tonight.'

'I'm going to pay a visit to four county commissioners in the very near future. If they give you Tobe's badge, you can investigate, amigo.'

Koonce shook hands with the others and as Ordway went deeper into the neat, little home to find Cartwright, Randolph told in detail of the burning of Pronghorn. When he finished Vernell asked a question.

'Was he always like this before he came home from Mexico?'

'Like what, ma'am?'

'Bitter. Hard. Merciless.'

'He burned the house where his mother died and where they brought the body of his father in a wagon. Nobody else would have, ma'am.'

'Do you think that possible subsequent extenuating circumstances might make him change his mind about burning our place?'

'I doubt it,' he answered in his quiet way.

She felt like stomping her booted foot in exasperation. Anger flared in her. 'But if you're appointed sheriff what will you do to prevent it?'

'Let's cross that bridge when we come to it, ma'am.'

Presently Ordway returned with a string-wrapped package of food beneath one arm. Mrs. Whitehouse had prepared it while he spent a few short minutes with Kathy. He could still see the pitifully thin body, the fear-filled, pleading eyes staring up at him from the dark circles.

'How is she, Mr. Ordway?' Vernell asked.

'I told her Mike was putting her back to work in the bank, and I think that helped.'

'And her husband?'

'Lon Perry is sober and will stay on guard. We'll get him.'

'Could I see her?' the girl asked.

'I'm sure of it. Six months from now she'll be a new person and prettier in a more mature way.' He voiced the words simply because he believed. There was no other thought back of them, no desire to start all over again. Kathy was locked out of his mind in that way and always would be because the man who had loved her was a man of no yesterdays.

A sharp pang of jealousy knifed through Vernell. She felt guilty, feeling this way toward a sick, tragedy-stricken girl. But she was a woman and couldn't help it. She was falling in love with Channon Ordway, one of the terrible, gun-fighting, black Ordways.

She told herself that it was gratitude toward him for having pulled them out of a desperation-motivated situation at Pronghorn. His visit to the little family plot had uncovered one of many probable facets of his complex character.

Then she heard him speaking and all illusion vanished.

'Bob,' he told the ex-deputy, 'this tenderfoot outfit paid off my trail crew double to pull out on me. They cat-footed me with guns, and then turned my herd over to Sonny, working under Ethan's orders.'

'So, Chann?'

'If I was capable of cooking up a little pity for them for being so foolish it's wiped out because they Rocking R-stamped some of my cattle today while I was a prisoner.'

He turned to Randolph. 'Whatever you paid my trail crew in wages,' he said coolly, 'take it out of my branded cattle at twenty dollars a head. Beyond a pair of chafed wrists I owe you nothing.'

'I believe I apologized for that,' Randolph replied stiffly.

'I burned one ranch tonight,' Ordway said as Doc Cartwright came up. 'I'll burn another one if necessary.'

'Here, here,' Cartwright snorted. 'What's all this talk?'

Ordway, however, accompanied by Koonce, was already moving through the night toward the black mare. Cartwright directed his shrewd gaze upon Mrs. Randolph.

She said in quiet resignation: 'Two stubborn men who should be friends instead of this way. We made a mistake, a terrible mistake. We wronged Mr. Ordway in a manner that leaves me ashamed.'

'He's a hard son-of-a-gun,' Doc admitted. 'But he'll soften up come time. His father did.'

'Regardless of any mistakes,' Randolph cut in with edged determination that Doc secretly knew was stubbornness, 'I still conduct the affairs of the valley according to my own best judgment.'

'And in the meantime,' Vernell asked, 'just what are two mere women supposed to do, Doctor?'

Over the cigar clamped in a corner of his mouth he gave her a look that was positively wicked. 'Why don't you try marrying the son-of-a-gun? His mother didn't do so bad with Tim,' he added a little softly.

She almost fled up the walk between the new flower beds, her face aflame, vowing that she would never understand these people and didn't ever again wish to try.

At the black mare Ordway was busy fastening the food inside Step's saddle bags. He and Koonce talked in low tones. Doc strolled up, cigar glowing, and Mike Adkins appeared hurriedly. Mike carried his old rifle in hand.

'They've just hit town, Chann,' he said hurriedly in a low voice. 'They're in Hanse's place and Ethan is a raving madman. God, he's gone crazy!'

'Not used to being bucked,' Ordway grunted, busy with rawhide thongs.

'What're you going to do?' Mike asked. His white hair shone like silver under the

Milky Way.

'Bob will tell you. Get word to the county commissioners and tell them it's either me or Ethan, and to take their choice about an acting sheriff. Do the best you can about protecting those women. In addition to being a block of ice, that damned Randolph is the most bullheaded man I ever ran into.'

'Look who's saying it!' jeered Doc Cartwright.

Ordway made no reply. He swung into the saddle. It was time to go, time to run for it.

No fox yet had ever turned on the hounds and emerged alive.

## CHAPTER TEN

Ordway swung into Step Eaton's saddle. He caught a glimpse of Randolph and his wife standing together alone. The aloof man wanted it that way. In the dim doorway glow, he saw also upon Mrs. Randolph's heart-shaped face the love and loyalty and yet the pain, the unhappiness that love and that loyalty were exacting.

He rode into the night and both Mike

and Doc came over. 'I don't trust that man insofar as my ranch is concerned,' Randolph stated distinctly. 'Very few of you people have given me reason to. He's a wes—'

'What do you plan to do about it?' Mike wanted to know, edgedly.

'Protect it,' came the crisp reply.

'Dammit, Eric,' Mike said exasperatedly. 'People in this country were just beginning to like you. They're just now beginning to forgive you for being the Hermit's brother. Don't ruin it by making Chann's job harder.'

'I'm still master of my own affairs,' Mike was reminded stonily.

'And what does that mean?' the banker asked sarcastically.

'I'll take my wife and niece to Rocking R and protect what is mine.'

'Oh Lord!' groaned Mike Adkins and threw up both hands, one of them rifle-weighted. 'For two cents, I'd have you roped and hog-tied. Hey, Bob.'

But Koonce had vanished in the night on foot, stalking the saloon to see what was going on in Hanse's place.

As for Ordway, Step's saddle didn't fit his seat nor his legs, and his Mexican boots felt strange not being shoved into bull-snout taps. He wanted his own equipment and was swinging around to Ethan's livery to see if it was there.

Somebody had pulled it from the dead horse, cleaned the blood away, and put it over a saddle rail beneath a shed. Swiftly he switched saddles and the food pack. The mare had travelled about twenty-five miles today, he guessed, but he knew she would be good for a few more tonight.

Somewhere in the night a couple of horses could be heard loping. Ordway paused under the shed, his eyes straining across to the store building. He saw two dim shapes clatter into view from Hansen's south porch and gallop across the fifty yard space.

Sonny's voice came clearly. 'I'd give a hundred dollars to know where Step is right now and what he's got in mind.'

'All right,' laughed the other. 'Maybe I could put a bullet in Hanse's big belly and make him talk before he cashed in his chips.'

Ordway strained his ears for the answer. It was drowned out by the black mare. Before he could grab her satiny nose she lifted it and shrilled a harridan's call to the two mounts from which Sonny and another range tough were dismounting.

'Hey!' exclaimed Shackleford in a low voice. 'That sounds a whole lot like that horse-hungry black bitch who's been losing a chunk of my money to Mike Adkins.'

'You can get it back from his bank anytime.'

'Shut up, damn you!' hissed Sonny. They started across the corral and Ordway slowly eased himself into the saddle a foot at a time.

'Hey, Lon!' Sonny whispered cautiously. 'Lon! You around?'

'Course he ain't,' scoffed the other, loudly. 'He's home with all the neighbors, braggin' about what a fine, upstandin' son-in-law he's got.'

Ordway dug in the round rowels and a four-footed black thunderbolt exploded from beneath the shed. She landed sprinting and a wild startled yell went up from one of the two men on the ground. A gun boomed and then another.

Ordway fired a shot at one figure and then the other, but which one was Sonny he didn't know. The two lances of orange flame slanted downward. More pistol reports went booming into the blackness and then Ordway was gone.

Sonny Shackleford stood cursing futilely, his yellow-flecked eyes flaming. From the ground at his feet came gurgling groans as a man twisted and writhed and threshed his legs in the final throes of death. A spur lashed convulsively against Sonny's ankle. It sent a poker-hot stab of flame through the bone and Sonny cursed the dying man.

He was still standing there spraddle-legged in the corral, eyes flaming with hatred, when Ethan and the others arrived at a run. Ethan's gaunt frame came towering through the night.

'Sonny!' he called.

'Right here,' Sonny snarled, and told what had happened. 'He musta thought John was me. He guessed wrong by three feet. Ethan, we've got to spread out and get him or he'll cut us down with that long range Sharps. One at a time.'

'Of course he will, you young fool. So why play his game? I think I know what he's planning to do. Let him do it. Then I'll toss the bait and let him come right into the trap.'

★     ★     ★

Ordway on the swift-footed mare was already out of town and down below the north rim of Squaw Valley. He knew what he was going to do, had intended setting out as soon as he burned Pronghorn. But the unexpected presence of the Randolphs had forced him to return to Tulac, to return them to the protection of Bob Koonce. He had some riding to do but some latent instinct was taking him first to the Rocking R.

Step Eaton was somewhere out here in the night. He didn't dare to be seen in Tulac. Even Mike or Hanse would shoot him down. He would be shocked sober, but his nerves would be raw and screaming for whiskey. And where would he find it?

At the Randolph place, even if he had to take it at the point of a gun.

'My God!' Channon Ordway suddenly spoke aloud, and a cold chill went along his spine. 'In the living room today. Step heard me say I'd burn that place out!'

He rolled in the silver spurs. 'All right, you horse-hungry black bitch,' he said to the mare as wind began to lash at his face. 'Now run, damn you!'

He was three miles away when he saw

that he had guessed right, and guessed too late. An orange glow was beginning to light up the sky, expanding ominously like a great new moon rising swiftly. The Hermit's architectural monstrosity was afire.

It was easy to guess what had happened. Step had circled the place like a red-eyed wolf, noticed the absence of window lights too early in the evening, and broken in.

It was another good guess that not until he was in the high-ceilinged white living room, on the spot where he had suffered humiliation and terror, going over in his mind the scene, that Chann's words had suddenly exploded in his liquor-soaked, hate-filled brain.

Ordway arrived on the panting mare. The eight or nine minaret-type turrets were buried in a great pillar of fire at least one hundred and fifty feet high.

The Randolphs, much of their family fortune squandered by the Hermit, their cattle stolen by Ethan Ordway, their bank funds exhausted, their home torched; the Randolphs were wiped out. Randolph was at least partly to blame.

Ordway circled the ranch in search of Step but found no trace. The back-shooter had fled into the night. Ordway sat there and watched the fire. Somewhere out there in the night one of his cattle bawled.

He wondered if it bore the rawly burned Rocking R stamp.

A few minutes later the Randolphs themselves arrived.

He didn't turn his head as they rode up. He didn't want to face them, to answer, to explain. Nor did they speak. There was no sound but the distant crackle of flames from that tall pillar of fire.

A new sound came to Channon Ordway's ears. The sound of a woman crying. Only twice in his life had he ever been affected by it. The first time had been when they brought home in a wagon to Pronghorn the body of Tim Ordway, after the gun fight in Hanse's saloon in which Ethan had come out alive. Ordway could still remember the small, choked sounds of a woman who also had lost everything. His mother.

The second one had been Kathy, on the day he had left for Mexico. She hadn't wanted him to go.

Channon Ordway turned his head and saw Vernell. She sat with her face in hands, shoulders shaking, and every choked sound that came out of her must have been a knife slash at every nerve, every breath, every emotion in her body. All the hopeless agony in a woman's soul came from those muffled, mewling sounds.

Mrs. Randolph was more composed. She sat erect in the saddle, looking short and stubby in the flickering light, tears making wet streaks down the cheeks of her heart-shaped face. She stared woodenly, straight ahead.

Eric Randolph's face was icy, composed. No emotion was upon it, nothing in the icy eyes back of the steel-rim spectacles. Now he turned and looked at Channon Ordway.

'Are you responsible for this?' he asked in a calm voice.

'Yes,' Ordway said. 'I burned it with my big mouth.'

'There's only one reason why I didn't kill you when we rode up. I am hoping you'll kill your uncle.'

Ordway lifted the reins and looked at him, at the two women. He said equally calmly, 'Since this afternoon in Tulac there has been some doubt in my mind that he is my uncle. It is my guess that he probably is my father. By brutal rape. I think that's the reason why my mother fled the house the night I was born, and came here, in order not to desecrate it.'

He left them there and rode out, eastward into the night. He climbed the tiring black mare up over the east crest and left the valley behind. The night swallowed him.

★     ★     ★

Two afternoons later, and about eighty miles or so to the east, Channon Ordway reached his destination. He was in country more virgin than that whence he came, a vast panorama of mesas and crags, and creeks sometimes hundreds of feet below.

The flat, grassy valley snuggled below more of the serrated crests rarely bare of snow until midsummer. He had ridden two days to ask an aged Indian where Ethan Ordway would bring a herd of cattle stolen a couple of dozen at a time. He had found the herd itself.

Around him as he rode through the tall grass were frolicking and sleeping spring calves. Others stood with forefeet spread wide to get lower under their mammies, tails twisting in ecstacy while they tugged milk from mothers bearing the Pronghorn brand. Ethan had made no effort to blot out or change the Rocking R.

About twenty Indian curs came yelping, as Ordway reached the village and pulled up before an emaciated old man of at least eighty. White Buffalo extended a thin hand and there was pleasure in the still clear eyes.

There was no talk inside the tepee until the pipe was lit and the usual words spoken, with appropriate gestures in six directions:

'The Sky is my father and the Earth is my mother. To the East, the Giver of Light. To the South, the Bringer of Warmth. To the West, the Thunder of the Rain Clouds. To the North, the Great Cleanser.'

That done, Ordway accepted some really good beef stew and got down to business with the old man.

'You've been gone a long time,' the old man said.

'I was supposed to be dead in Mexico.'

'That's what the white men said.'

'You knew better?'

'I knew,' the ancient one replied.

'Why did you accept the stolen cattle my uncle brought last summer?'

'To keep them for you. But you've come

145

alone.'

'I'll need some help, my father. Twenty of the young men from over on the reservation . . .'

At day break the following morning, twenty young Ute bucks dressed mostly in old hats, brush jumpers, blue denim pants and moccasins started the Randolph cattle on the return journey west. It was a bawling mass of confusion that first day, a little better the second day, and after that the drive became slow routine.

Ordway himself took no active part in the drive. With all those little calves along, it was less a cattle drive and more like herding a band of sheep. The Utes knew their business and were patient. They considered this not work but an opportunity to break up the boredom of dull reservation life.

Ordway's work lay in the surrounding country. He had to know what, if anything, Ethan intended doing while the cattle and the new calves were being returned to the home range.

Mounted upon one shaggy Indian pony after another, and often riding the fleet, black mare, his was the role of the hunter. He rode circle daily; grim, unshaved, wary.

By now he was convinced that Ethan had no intention of molesting the herd. But too much was at stake, including Ordway's life, to cease vigilance.

Day after day the herd moved along, averaging about seven or eight miles between suns. Yet by the time it had covered half of the eighty miles to Pronghorn Basin, Ordway knew that somebody was playing shadow. It might be Step. It could be some skulking member of Sonny's bunch to watch and report progress. It could be the tawny young tough himself, although this was doubtful.

For two or three more days Ordway played cat-and-mouse with a man who knew his business. Once he caught sight of the man on a distant knoll all of a thousand yards away. At another time Ordway had closed in to within five hundred yards when the skulker's horse vanished into the brush clump of a ravine.

'Real smart one, huh?' Ordway grunted. 'Trying to pull me into an ambush maybe.'

Still the fellow's actions were at times puzzling. Well, it didn't matter much now. Up ahead was a spring where he and Koonce had camped many times during hunting trips of past years. If Bob could get away from Tulac he'd be there tomorrow night. If not, he'd try to leave a message. Meanwhile, the time had come to tie a knot or two in that skulking horseman's short-tail.

That evening when camp was made, Ordway went to old White Buffalo. He told the old man that the herd was in no danger of attack and stampede and that the posting of unarmed guards would no longer be necessary. White Buffalo nodded and said that was good. His people wanted no trouble.

At daybreak the following morning Ordway saddled the black mare. She was rested and aching for a run. In the first gray of dawn as the mist-wet leaves hung limp and lifeless, Ordway began riding circle near the head of the bedded down herd, eyes on the wet grass. Trailing was second nature to him, and, sure enough, the emboldened skulker had sneaked in closer than usual during the dark hours!

Not very long ago either, judging from the amount of dew in the tracks. Ordway swung back into the saddle, turned around and rode carelessly back east, the way he had come. Once out of sight, however, he broke the long winded mare into a muscle-warming trot and then a lope. He went a mile south. Then another mile. Now he swung the mare west and began to stretch her out hard. She ran like a she-demon out of hell, effortlessly.

For seven hard miles he drove her. After letting her blow for a few minutes he now headed her north again, crossing an open space more than a mile across. Game trails ranged the length of this, and it would be the logical route for the skulker to follow while keeping ahead of the herd.

By the time Ordway crossed to the other side there was a look of grim satisfaction on his face for the first time in days. His man hadn't reached here yet. He'd been circled and cut off.

Channon Ordway dismounted under cover. Squatting on his heels he built a cigarette. A jay scolded noisily above his head and the sun worked its warmth deeper into his shoulders. He rubbed a work-hardened finger over his face and discovered that all scabs from Red Waldo's blows had healed and fallen away.

His eyes were watching the grassy expanse for two miles east.

A big buck deer, with a magnificent cluster of prongs, came up out of a hidden draw where he'd hid out near water all night. A cagey old fellow, that one. It was why no hunter or wolf pack had cut him down. He'd go up above where the timber afforded protection, grazing and sleeping all day, and he wouldn't be down for water until just before sundown.

Ordway's saddle creaked as the black mare swung her head. He leaped just in time and grabbed her nose. 'Oh, no you don't!' he grunted at her.

The rider had emerged from a motte not more than two hundred yards away. He rode leisurely, leaving a plain trail. He was looking back over one shoulder every couple of minutes, and grinning as though at some huge joke. He was Harl Griddle, a middle-aged cow thief, and no killer.

A few minutes later, when he turned around, he found himself facing a black apparition. Ordway sat the mare with the deadly Sharps in his hands, cocked and half way to his shoulder.

'Just keep on coming,' he called from fifty yards away. 'I want in on the joke.'

The man obeyed. The grin was gone from his face. It was as blank as it had been the day he'd watched Channon Ordway kill Jude Waldo in a gun fight in Cheyenne.

'What's funny, Harl?' Channon asked him.

'Shucks now, Chann,' Harl replied. 'I wasn't laughin' at you. I was laughin' at Ethan. He's had me down here for a week to keep an eye on the herd and let him know how it's comin'.'

'And that's supposed to be funny, huh?'

'You don't savvy,' grinned the other. 'He paid me one hundred extra, easiest money I ever made. Leastwise doin' honest work.'

'I can save you anymore trouble,' Ordway said. 'Just tell him I'm putting the cattle in Pronghorn for the present.'

'I'll shore do that,' the other said, relief showing in his face. 'You want me to go now?'

'Where is Ethan?' Ordway asked.

'Headquarterin' in Hanse's saloon. Not very welcome either. People are some riled up the way you burned out the Rockin' R. Then when Ethan appointed Sonny as sheriff, and put the Rockin' R up for tax sale tomorrow they really riled!'

Ordway sat dumbfounded for a few moments. You should have known, Chann. You should have remembered that Ethan never made a move in his life unless he had an ace or two up his sleeve. He's not only taking Squaw Valley legally, but you're driving Randolph's own cattle back and putting them in Ethan's hands on Ethan's Pronghorn range!

'What happened to the Randolphs?' Ordway demanded.

The cow thief shrugged his burly shoulders. 'Faded. Gone. Vamoosed.' Harl shrugged again. 'Nobody knows.'

'Where's Step?'

'No sabe. Some say he might have left the country.'

'Where's Koonce?'

'Around. But it's a dozen rifles against a Greener if he tries to leave town.'

Ordway let the man go, and rode toward the herd, frowning. There was something about this that didn't fit. Ethan wanted him dead and intended that it would be so. But not now apparently. With Ordway dead the unarmed Utes would scatter like quail and then Ethan would have a trail drive on his hands.

Ordway shook his head and rode on. Later he heard a faint rifle shot.

Late that afternoon, riding an Indian pony now, he left the two stolid Utes riding point, after giving them instructions about a bed ground. Tonight would be the last one. Tomorrow the herd of almost four thousand head of cows and calves would spill in a red tide over the east brink of Pronghorn and spread out to luxuriate in the basin's green carpet.

Well, he remembered. He had promised Eric Randolph in those first minutes of their odd meeting that he would try to find out who had stolen the man's cattle and where they were. He had kept his word. He had more than made good his promise.

He had brought the stolen herd to home country again. To Ethan!

At the back of the herd, he saw a wagon different from the one old White Buffalo's family used. This was a small, canvas topped affair and Ordway was momentarily puzzled until he rode closer and recognized the team. They didn't look like sleek surrey horses now. They were tired, dusty. The wagon was the kind that Eric Randolph would have brought hurriedly at some small out-of-the-way ranch, with little time to bargain. It rocked along from side to side and appeared to contain nothing but the barest necessities of camp life.

Mrs. Randolph was driving and Vernell rode close by.

But Eric Randolph was not within sight.

# CHAPTER ELEVEN

The older woman sat upright in the spring seat with gloved hands holding the reins. She was guiding the team around rocks and over rain-leached cuts in the terrain. From inside the canvas came the melancholy bawl of calves.

Little fellows too new born and weak to stay up.

It was hard to picture this woman as having three impish young sons in an exclusive school several thousand miles away. Yet in the great melting pot of the west you found derby'd road agents who were educated gentlemen and apprehensive lest they frighten the lady passengers. You saw a cowpuncher playing Schubert melodies on the beat up keys of a saloon piano.

And people had seen Ellen Ordway as a new bride on the ranch in Pronghorn Basin. She had come to a Colorado wilderness with Tim Ordway, as Mary Randolph had gone to India with her aristocratic husband.

The two women pulled up and waited

when they saw Ordway approach. He couldn't tell whether they still believed he had burned their home that night last week, but they appeared uncertain and yet with a determination characteristic of Randolph himself. Ordway reined in close beside the left front wheel and touched a hand to the brim of his sombrero.

'I'm taking it for granted that we are not welcome, Mr. Ordway,' Vernell said steadily. 'But in some respects we had no choice.'

There were tired lines around Mrs. Randolph's eyes where last he had seen a steady flow of quiet grief, but there was nothing antagonistic in the glance she gave him. She seemed beyond hatred. Or most likely, he told himself, she never learned how.

'You look a bit tired,' he remarked smilingly.

The older woman removed her hat and smiled back faintly. 'Not more so than perhaps Eric is.'

'With apologies to two courageous women, certainly not as damned stubborn.' Ordway's own smile faded. He was remembering that faint rifle shot. 'Where is he?'

She waved a vague hand. 'Out there someplace, I guess. He followed your trail the day after . . . the fire, and then hurried home. We were aware by then that all three of us were in equal danger. We've been hidden out until he located the herd today and told Vernell and myself to join you.'

'All right. We're on our last camp before hitting Pronghorn Basin tomorrow. Camp site is a half mile ahead and a bit south at a spring.'

He touched his hat brim again and loped away to select a calfless heifer for butchering by the Utes. A new uneasiness he had concealed from the woman now assailed him. Randolph certainly had used his head in getting his wife and niece out of danger.

Now the damned, lofty-prided fellow had put them right back into danger, not to mention the cattle, and gone off on his own.

Every yard that the herd now advanced closer to Pronghorn lessened their need for his guidance and brought larger over him the shadow of ambush. He now didn't dare to ride within five hundred yards of a motte or ravine lip for fear it contained a rifleman like Step. And if Ordway went down out of the saddle and the unarmed Utes scattered in panic, those two women likely would be killed as ruthlessly as Sonny had shot the two young squaws.

'Damned bullheaded stiff-neck,' Ordway growled darkly. If the man had only locked his superciliousness toward the natives in a closet and made friends... If only he hadn't been so distant and aloof...

Ordway's uneasiness for the man's safety grew. Harl Griddle was no killer in the sense that he'd shoot it out when the odds were even. But there had been a rifle on his saddle, Ethan wanted Randolph dead, and if he got a shot at the man's back he'd take it without hesitation.

'If Randolph just keeps fooling around long enough,' Ordway went on growling to himself, 'he's going to find out that playing hunter is a little different when the game is armed with a good Winchester instead of a pair of claws. The effective range is a little different too!'

He remembered again the sound of that distant rifle shot, and his uneasiness for the safety of Eric Randolph, of the two women, grew.

It was shortly after dark that evening when Ordway scratchingly finished whittling off a murderous-looking crop of black bristle and put on the damp shirt he'd hand washed below the spring and hung out to dry. The nights were turning warmer and the stars winked brightly. The herd was bedded down and all bawling ceased as the last mother found the last lost calf.

The Indian guards were out, but they carried no arms. All they could do in case of attack would be to yell a warning.

Ordway took a long-bladed sheath knife from his cantle roll and rose. The freshly butchered beef carcass, a night-wandering trouble maker that would butt no more cows awake, hung from a large limb nearby. From the Indian fires a hundred yards away came the smell of raw beef over camp fire coals. He thought of the food Mrs. Ordway had prepared in the kitchen that other day—when he had acted such a boor, and his stomach cried out a protest at such impiety.

A light step sounded behind him. It gave off a crisp sound in the spring night. He didn't whirl with a gun out. He knew the sound and it made his heart leap. He had heard it the first time when Eric Randolph covered him with a sporting gun and Vernell stepped into view. Even then sight of her had made his hungry blood pound. Now he was unashamedly glad.

He knew at that moment that he loved this strange girl very, very much.

Not as he had loved Kathy Perry. That had been different. She had been an ex-outlaw's child, one of his own kind. She'd received a modicum of education in the crude facilities Tulac's little group of people had afforded, and much of her life had been occupied carrying a new baby brother or sister on an out-thrust hip. About the time she was eleven or twelve Ordway had come upon her just as Sonny had her down in a weed patch with most of her clothing torn off, and Sonny had taken a terrible beating from a bigger and older Channon. When she was about fifteen, and Step, a big lout and drinking now at eighteen, also got roughly amorous one night, Step, too, took a terrible beating.

After that everybody understood that it was just a question of time until Kathy Perry grew up and Channon Ordway made up his mind to settle down. The town drunkard's daughter was going to come out all right!

That was the way it had been. That was the way it was not anymore, and never could be again. That was what he was remembering as he saw this girl, Vernell Randolph.

As this same day earlier, she stood a bit uncertain. She knew he had made good his threat to burn their ranch, just as the next moment she knew it couldn't be so. She knew that he must resent their presence here like homeless neighbors seeking shelter and charity. Events of the past eight days had burned harshly into her, had drained away the usual spirited asperity. Had he been right that first day? Eric turning desperate man hunter; Mary over there on her knees beside a cook fire; and herself . . . Had the fiber begun to coarsen?

She hesitated as though seeking a way to break the barrier that ever had been between them from the first moment they met.

He spotted the hesitation and did it for her. 'You just made a picture for a moment I'll be a long time forgetting, Vernell,' using her name for the first time. 'Welcome to the camp of the enemy.'

The bright spots appeared in her cheeks again and a strange kind of pain appeared in the unusual onyx eyes. 'Please,' she said in a low voice. 'My aunt Mary invites you to share our food. The beggars offering to share their little with those who have more.'

He sheathed the big knife and walked over to her. She knew what was going to happen and was powerless to protest, to prevent it. His mouth came down upon hers and she was amazed to find it warm, gentle; tender. She stood woodenly, but a quiver ran through her lithe body and when she stepped back she knew there was a near panic in her eyes.

She looked at him like some wild thing that was cornered, trapped; paralyzed and unable to flee. 'Don't,' she got out huskily. 'Please, you mustn't ever do that again . . . Channon Ordway.'

'If the time ever comes I feel you mean it, I won't,' he said gently.

They walked to where the canvas topped wagon was dimly outlined in the light of the fire. Mrs. Randolph, spoon in hand, stood staring off into the night toward the west. Now she turned with a smile of welcome.

'I was simply hoping that I might hear the sound of Eric's mount. Mr. Ordway, what we have hardly will be on par with the last food I had the pleasure of serving you. But we'll do our best.'

He grinned with new feeling.

'My name is Channon, Mrs. Randolph, and after the manners I displayed that day to spite Vernell, you should have thrown me out of the house.' His face sobered. 'It might sound a little strange to you, Mrs. Randolph, but I've been considerably concerned about the picture.'

She looked puzzled. He added: 'The one of the three boys. In the kitchen. Did you save it?'

She shook her head. 'No, Mr.—Channon. It was on Eric's secretary in the big room.'

'If I had burned your home like I foolishly threatened,' he said slowly, 'I would have given you back that picture tonight.'

She looked embarrassed and a flush appeared in her rounded cheeks. A new light had come into Vernell's own face. 'You never burned our home, did you, Channon?' she cried out.

He shook his head.

★    ★    ★

The food was like manna from heaven after the Mexican camp fare he'd been used to for months, plus a week of his own and Indian cooking. He stopped eating only because good manners dictated it.

'There's quite a legend among many about old Kit Carson, one of our fabulous mountain men who once wintered where Tulac now stands,' he sighed, leaning back against a wagon wheel. 'After months in the wilderness he went into a dining room in San Francisco, ordered five meals, and ate them all. Now I know how he felt.'

A strange, brief contentment came over him as he leaned back and built a cigarette. Now he realized more than ever what marriage had done for Tim Ordway, what too much loneliness had done to Ethan Ordway. A man needed a woman and a goal in life. Without it he was nothing.

A couple of hundred yards away some of the younger Ute bucks, still overflowing with restive energy, had built themselves a separate, larger fire. They'd brought out a couple of drums and now were hammering away while they pranced around the fire and kyoodled by way of the usual evening amusement. Mrs. Randolph, dish-drying towel in hand, listened for a few moments and then turned her worried face to the west again and the darkness out there.

163

Ordway said, 'Did he say when he'd be back?'

'He is so precise, Channon,' she nodded. 'It's his way of life, the same manner in which people out here consider him cold and aloof. If we could only have remained here long enough as peaceful cattle raisers. With no murder of his wayward brother, no theft of our cattle, people would have seen a warm and friendly man, eager to be of service to the community.'

Ordway got to his feet and pinched out the cigarette butt. 'What time did he expect to return, Mrs. Randolph,' he asked slowly.

'About dusk, Channon. He was planning to make the ride to Tulac and return. He wanted to slip into town and have a talk with Mr. Koonce.'

Ordway thought of Harl. Ten to one Randolph had cut his trail within a mile or two after meeting Ordway. Or, vice versa, that rifle shot. Chances were that one of those two men was dead. He should have investigated.

Ordway controlled his feelings. 'I wish I had known that.'

'You think something serious may have happened?' Vernell asked anxiously from on her knees beside the dishpan.

'The last thing I told Koonce the night I left Tulac,' he explained, 'was that I was coming east eighty miles to old White Buffalo's little village on the edge of the reservation. Ethan hadn't sold any cattle of yours in either Denver or Cheyenne. Mike Adkins would have known about it. So chances were that he was holding over there, waiting for the calves to be weaned before selling the cows to the agency for fall beef. It turned out to be a good guess.

'Figuring six or eight miles a day on the return trip, Bob was supposed either to be here tonight or let me know what was going on, or leave a message on a ledge above the spring, where we built our campfires. There was no message and so far he hasn't shown up.

'I've been trying to tell myself for the past three hours that nothing is wrong. Now I know better. If Eric Randolph doesn't show up by midnight, I'm going to Tulac and I can't leave you here without protection. We'll leave about midnight.'

He strode into the night. Had he not been too preoccupied he would have noticed that the beat of the drums had changed. So had the kyoodling of the young bucks. There was something no longer carefree in the sound. It had become ominous, and now it suddenly ceased.

At the fire two women looked at each other, no words necessary to express the sickening fear that Randolph might no longer be alive. Then the girl's eyes took in the tall gun-belted figure in *vaquero* clothing who had kissed her. It did something to her face. Unknown to her, Mary Randolph saw and guessed.

'You're in love with Channon, aren't you kitten?' she asked, using her and Eric's pet name for the girl they considered more of a daughter than niece.

'Yes,' Vernell nodded. 'But when he kissed me tonight I don't think it was love. I just happened to be the first available woman within reach to help drown his disappointment over the loss of Kathy Eaton.'

## CHAPTER TWELVE

At midnight Ordway saddled two good horses and the black mare. She was no longer in fear of a fist smash in the face from Step when he was drunk, or after she lost a sprint race. But there were a number of knothead Indian pony scrub studs in the Ute *remuda*, and Ordway had taken no chances. He kept her on picket and curried her, hoping that some day in the future he could use her as the nucleus of a fine band of racers.

Old White Buffalo, a sixty-year, moth-eaten white robe from an albino buffalo around his skinny shoulders, stood nearby. Leading the mare, Channon went over and stuck out his hand.

'We are going now, my father. Put the herd in Pronghorn Basin tomorrow and then return home. If I do not come to you with money in two weeks, there will be no pay.'

'There was blood on the clouds at sundown, and a coyote ran up a tree that had no limbs.'

The old man withdrew his limp brown claw from Ordway's hand and looked up at the sky. Likely he was sending out his thought spirits and asking them for a safe journey for the three whites, Ordway guessed.

Ordway leathered aboard the satiny mare and rode over to where Vernell and Mary

Randolph waited. He set a course due west beneath the Big Dipper. One of the horses slobbered and to his tautened nerves it sounded louder than that rifle shot. He kept thinking about Harl Griddle and why Ethan hadn't sent Step or Sonny or a good long-gun expert. Why had he sent a harmless middle-aged man who'd let himself fall into Ordway's trap.

Ethan had wanted to impart some information to Ordway. He had used Griddle to do it. He had wanted Ordway to know about the tax auction and that Sonny was sheriff.

The whole thing had been too easy. To kill him out here, Ordway surmised, might scare the Randolphs away again.

He had wanted to make certain that Channon would arrive in town at the precise day of Ethan's choosing, on a day when he would obtain legal control of Squaw Valley for a probable one dollar bid, and kill him ruthlessly.

Kill him and clean the town of any other person who stood in his way. Information about the tax sale had been the bait.

'You've been quiet for too long,' Vernell's voice finally came from beside him. 'Is there something worrying you?'

He told the two women riding on either side of him about Harl Griddle. 'Ethan figured that you folks were either with the herd or in touch with me, after you disappeared. He wanted Randolph to know about the sheriff's tax sale. He's been sitting in town like a big black spider, drawing us both into the trap.'

He made no mention of the rifle shot, but his course was directed to where he had met the middle-aged cow thief. They came to the spot, the motte a dark blob in the night. Ordway guided a little farther to the north-west, and pulled down to a walk. Another half mile. And then a mile. It should be somewhere in this vicinity, the place where he had heard the shot . . .

The black mare's nose didn't let him down. He heard the nervous slobber and then she shied over against Mrs. Randolph's horse. 'Stay here,' he said in a low voice.

'You think . . .'

'I don't know. I'm just hoping.'

He got down and led the nervous mare forward. Within a hundred yards he found the body. He lit a match and looked down. Griddle, the lifetime cow thief and oldest member of Sonny's outfit, lay on his back with one arm outspread. His hat was off and his face lay in flabby repose. His rifle was nearby. He'd been shot through the chest.

The two women had seen the flare of the match and now rode up as Ordway picked up the dead man's old repeater. 'It's all right,' he called. 'It's Harl Griddle.'

'Thank God,' came a murmured reply from Mary. 'Harl. Yes, I remember the name now. But, Channon, what could have become of my husband?'

He examined the gun, a six-shot with four in the magazine. There was another in the chamber. Five. One shot probably fired. Had it killed Eric Randolph?

'It's too dark for tracking and we've got to get into town before daybreak. All you can do is hope ... and maybe a little praying.'

They reached Pronghorn and descended the east side of the basin. They picked their way across the floor, through the lush grass, at a horse-saving jog. They passed a mile away and to the left of a distant pile of ashes and some ancient corrals and sheds and other crude buildings, and rode on. They came again to the grassy mound and the white picket fence, but did not stop.

Again Vernell spoke through the night. 'Tell me something, Channon. When we first came here, Eric, trying to be friendly then, asked Ethan Ordway why Squaw Valley had been so named. Ethan almost struck him. If it's not too personal—'

'It's been a long time ago now to everybody except Ethan. It must have eaten into him like cancer all these years. My mother chose Tim instead of him because Tim was a gentleman sucked into outlawry out of loyalty to his brother. On the night I was due to be born Tim fought through the snow storm to get Doc Cartwright rather than ask his brother to go. He was that kind of man. He couldn't get back and my mother fled the house and went to the little Indian camp where your home was.

'Next morning, when Ethan guessed where she'd gone and came after her with a wagon bed mounted on sled runners, she screamed and fought and had to be taken back by force. I guess that on the way home she calmed down and decided to live with her terrible secret. Anyhow, the Utes named the place, "Valley Where Squaw Was Angry," and pretty soon it was just Bitter Squaw Valley.'

He lapsed into silence once more, and the two women wisely left him alone with his thoughts; the knowledge that he was going to kill the man who had done this. His father.

They rode through a narrow cut separating Pronghorn from the north end of the valley. Below the bluffs on which the town sat, they crossed Rocking R's wagon road up a narrow cut, and circled around for a steeper trail climb into the west side of Tulac.

There were no guards to challenge them and the back of Kathy's house was over yonder in the darkness, two hundred yards away.

The time was shortly before dawn.

Near the house Ordway dismounted from the black mare and handed his reins to Vernell. 'If she starts to neigh,' he instructed in a whisper, 'Jerk her head up. I've got to see if anybody is on guard. Lon might have a nervous shotgun trigger finger.'

He left them and moved forward, Colt wary, and pulled up by Kathy's chicken coop. From it emanated a sleepy cluck or two. The house looked dark but his night-accustomed eyes told him finally that two

172

or three squares were lighter than the rest. Blankets over the windows.

'Hey, Lon,' he hissed.

'That you, Chann?' came Koonce's instant reply. 'Lordy, but I'm glad you got here.'

Ordway moved forward and shook hands in the night. 'I've got a couple of women who are very much worried about that strong-willed man of theirs.'

'They have good reason to be,' the ex-deputy answered cryptically.

'That bad?' Ordway asked and dreaded the reply.

'Damned near. I slid out of town today to keep the meeting with you. Ethan's bunch have let me alone so far, as long as I kept my nose out of their business. On the other side of the basin I found Randolph. He was done in. Shot bad and almost bled to death until he got his wound plugged with that scarf he always wore.'

Ordway told him about Harl Griddle. 'The way I got it figured their trails crossed and Harl figured Randolph for an easy kill. He must have been quite surprised when the Britisher put a quick one through his heart with a fancy rifle.'

'I had to get him back here to Doc, and

this was the only place to bring him. And I was spotted, of course. You know what that means.'

'Has anybody seen Step?'

'He's here, sober, and half crazy to see Kathy again except that Lon sleeps with a shotgun by his chair around the clock.' He handed Ordway the sawed-off shotgun. 'Here. I'll get the women. Go on in the kitchen and get yourself some coffee. Door is to the left and don't stumble over them washtubs.'

Ordway found the door and opened it. Light struck his face. He closed it and laid the shotgun on the table with checkered oilcloth top. A woman entered the room and he turned. It was Kathy.

*     *     *

For a woman who had miscarried but a little over a week ago Kathy had shown astounding recovery. She wore a light dress, and Ordway noted that she was pitifully thin. Not a pound over ninety, he guessed, and her stem-like neck looked like the bas-relief of one of those ancient Egyptian goddesses. He almost could have encircled it with the middle finger and

174

thumb of one hand.

However, the dark circles beneath her eyes were clearing, beginning to match the lighter texture of her smooth skin, and he knew it would be but a matter of time until she'd be healthy once more. Only one thing gave him concern. In her eyes, larger than he'd ever seen them in the old days, lay a haunting fear.

She knew that Step was back in Ethan's good graces because he had fired the Randolph ranch house. It was an open secret all over Tulac. She knew also that Step was sober, was temporarily contrite toward her for what had happened to an unborn baby , and that he wanted to start all over again.

If Ordway and Koonce went down under gunfire there would be no hope for her. The whole brutal cycle would start all over again.

She gave Ordway a wan smile and came closer, and a pity that was more of an older brother rose inside him. He took her in his arms and held her close. It was the kind of gesture he'd have done with a frightened child, a kicked puppy. In a certain sense he felt responsible for the tragedy she had suffered, and the pity arose anew as she snuggled against his chest.

'Oh, Chann, I'm scared,' she whispered in a muffled voice. 'Ethan and Sonny and Step are holed up over in Hanse's saloon. Mike is barricaded in his bank. Pete the barber is dead. Ethan shot him because he wouldn't give him a shave one night. Pa's been wonderful but he's nigh crazy for a few drinks. Chann! Chann! What are we going to do?'

It was thus that Vernell heard the last of it, and thus she found them when she stepped inside the kitchen. Ordway turned with the girl against his breast. He caught one glimpse of the terrible pain in the strange, dark eyes and his own heart almost collapsed. Any hopes he had now were gone.

Nothing on earth would ever convince the girl now but that he still loved Kathy, still intended to get her back.

Kathy blushed and pushed herself out of Ordway's arms and straightened the dress over her thin, almost emaciated body. Outside, a rooster, awakened by three horses tied at the coop, cocked its head back and crowed a salute to the morning.

And out there too one of the horses began to mouth at the loosely knit knot holding her to a post. The black mare was at it again.

'I'm so glad you're safe,' Kathy said breathlessly to the women. 'I guess Bob told you Mr. Randolph got shot. But he's in my bed and Doc Cartwright says he'll pull through. You got nothing to worry about.'

'I'm sure we haven't,' Mary Randolph replied murmuringly. 'And we're grateful for your kindness.'

'You come with me,' Kathy said and led the way.

Ordway went to a doorway and looked in. He caught a glimpse of a man half propped up among pillows. Randolph's eyes were closed and he was breathing heavily. Doc Cartwright motioned with his head and followed Ordway back to the kitchen.

'He's got guts, that fellow. How are you, boy?'

'What chance has he got, Doc?' Ordway asked and went to the stove for coffee.'

'Just a question of time until his distillery can cook up a new batch of blood,' the goateed little man replied. 'Too bad medical science can't figure out a way for me to pump about a gallon of new blood in

177

him. He'd be on his feet in no time.'

He accepted the coffee from Ordway and sat down tiredly, resting an elbow on the cloth. 'Wish I had some whiskey to spike this. I sure need a shot, but don't dare bring any in the house.'

'Lon?' Ordway asked, pouring for himself. He looked at Koonce, who shook his head and said, 'Had mine all night.'

Doc said, 'It's been years since he's gone this long without a drink. Now that Kathy is on the way to recovery all he needs is one good shot of liquor and you'd have to hog-tie him to keep him out of Hanse's.'

He drank moodily from the cup, not seeing it, eyes on the floor beyond. A tired sigh came up out of his lungs. 'One by one the old bunch are gradually slipping away. Now old Pete is gone. Your uncle is an insane mad dog, Chann.'

Ordway said quietly, 'I don't think he's my uncle, Henry. I'm convinced that Ethan is really my father.'

Doc looked only faintly startled. He put down his cup and the sigh rose once more from his tired lungs. 'Well. As long as you know, I'm glad I wasn't the one to tell you. Your mother shared that terrible secret with me the first time I came to look at you, and I think Ethan brooded about it so much his thinking became all twisted.'

His eyes turned hard and bright like lead-colored glass. His voice was pitched low so that those in the sick room might not overhear.

'So you might as well know what Hanse and Pete and me have known for twenty years, because we witnessed that gunfight. Ethan framed Tim into that shoot-out in Hanse's place.'

'There is a thing called instinct, and one called destiny,' Channon Ordway said. 'Perhaps that is why I knew a long time before it happened that someday I'd kill Red Waldo's brother. Go on, Doc.'

'Ethan,' Cartwright went on, 'hired young Jude Waldo and two other easy-money young toughs to come down here and get the drop on him in a supposed three-way brace. The idea was that Tim would jump in to help. And that's the way it worked out. When Tim jerked his six-shooter to save his brother, Ethan pulled the double cross he'd worked out with Waldo. He shot those other two young toughs to death, Jude centered his gunfire on Tim and killed him, and Ethan let Jude escape. He's a monster, Chann.'

There was silence in the kitchen for a few moments. Ordway had been seven years old when it all happened. Looking back, he could see how his mother had been literally a prisoner of Ethan on Pronghorn, or perhaps how she had grittily remained to see that her son came into his own.

It had taken five more years at the hands of Ethan, and an agony of sorrow and shame, before she had given way—something a twelve year old boy hadn't understood.

Outside in the coop the rooster stopped crowing and a few alarmed cackles arose as the mouthing black mare finally worked loose the wet reins.

Holding her head high and to one side to avoid stepping upon them, she moved away.

She was stud-hungry and she headed straight for Hanse's south porch where a number of other horses had been racked all night.

# CHAPTER THIRTEEN

The lights in Hanse's saloon were the only ones visible in the small town. The horses, exchanged at the livery at regular intervals in case anything went wrong, dozed outside. In the low interior of the place all was quiet except for the muted click of chips as four men silently played poker. Hanse was gone, had been gone since Ethan's insane killing of Pete. He'd pulled a six-shooter from beneath the bar, untied his apron with one hand, called Ethan a mad dog son-of-a-bitch, and backed out the side entrance to his place. Into his old cabin, the original saloon.

He was now holed up in the bank with Mike, in the latter's upstairs office. If Ethan had to run for it and needed some fast cash at the last minute, he was going to be in for one hell of a surprise!

A half-dozen or so of Sonny's men were asleep on the blankets scattered around the door. Nobody was drinking. Nobody had had a drink for forty-eight hours.

Wrapped in a buffalo robe, Ethan sat in Hanse's own comfortable chair at the open end of the bar. He looked like some great grizzly that had wandered in. His gun smashed face was not yet fully healed. His shaggy black hair hung down around it. But his eyes, despite lack of sleep lately, were clear; brooding.

He heard Sonny's low chuckle as he raked in a small pot from Step in the penny-ante game. Those two didn't quarrel anymore; partly because Ethan had so ordered it, but mostly because Step was sober and Sonny had sense enough not to push his jeers any further.

Only trouble with Step, though, was that woman of his. There weren't any loose women in Tulac, hadn't been for fifteen years. Not enough money. Except for maybe finding himself a young squaw now and then, Step had been womanless for months because of Kathy's pregnancy. Now she was going to be all right pretty soon and Ethan recognized the symptoms.

That was the trouble with a damn woman, Ethan reflected. She made a man contented. Take his brother, Tim . . .

He got up slowly and let the robe slide down around the chair. He looked at the spot there on the door where Tim had died that day twenty years ago. Memories came flooding back, things he'd forced out of his mind; other things over which he had brooded.

He went behind the bar and opened a bottle and poured himself a drink. The poker players looked up, and along one wall a man shoved aside blankets and raised himself up on an elbow and yawned.

'Bar's open for a few,' Ethan said. 'It'll be closed later.'

'Pour me one,' Sonny said and pushed back his chair.

'Step?' Ethan called.

Step shook his head. 'Good boy,' Ethan grinned. 'I just hope Lon goes down to the livery and finds that bottle we stashed in his favorite hiding place.'

Sonny came over and picked up his drink, pushing back his tawny locks with his other hand. 'So do I. It'll be one gun less if we have to rush the house. He can have his booze, I just want that girl!'

'He'll find it,' Ethan grinned. The drink went down smoothly and warmed his belly. He poured himself one more. Sonny's face broke into a scowl.

'You reckon that damned dude cashed in his chips after Bob brought him in?'

'Why don't you go over and ask Henry?'

Ethan chuckled with rare humor.

'I'm asking what's become of Harl?' Sonny snarled. 'He should have been back yesterday. Four men now. Four of my men dead and nine left, and not one damned sign that Chann took the bait!'

'He took it,' Ethan said. 'He's got more of my Ordway blood in him than he realizes, and the black Ordways were always good at thinking things out.'

He corked the bottle, hit the stopper with the palm of his hand, placed it on a shelf behind him, and came out from back of the bar. He walked toward the south entrance and came out upon the roofless porch.

He stood there, looking at the stars. They were shimmering, but fast losing their twinkle. Roosters were crowing all over town. A haze that looked almost like a fog hung over the valley rim as well as Pronghorn, and the thought came to him suddenly that he had never had time to enjoy all this the way Doc had. Doc with his paint brushes and oil colors and canvases always in the back of the buggy.

He found himself strangely moved by the silence and the beauty. For a few moments it all came home to him, the wasted years, the hatreds, and the violent passions that drew no line of decency toward his brother's wife, no line of blood toward his own brother.

He shook off the mood and the old one came back and he scowled. Women. They were always making trouble. He turned as the sound of dainty hoofs came clicking on the hard packed earth. To his amazement he saw Step's black mare. She came up with reins dragging, carrying a Mexican saddle, and nuzzled one of the dozing horses.

Ethan Ordway took one look down yonder past where his livery was located, looked in the darkness beyond it toward Step's home. A hard grin broke his black-whiskered features.

'I knew it,' he breathed softly. 'I knew it! He's all Ordway.'

He turned around and went back inside. The game had broken up. Sonny was idly dealing himself a hand of solitaire. Ethan looked around.

'Where's Step?' Ethan asked sharply.

'Why,' Sonny replied in surprise, 'I reckon he must have stepped outside.'

He leaped to his feet and ran to the north door, gun in hand. He saw the dark figure

185

forty feet away and called softly. 'Turn around, Step. Slow and easy. Now come back.'

They came back inside. Ethan said mildly, 'Chann's here. Your black mare is out front. Just in case you had any ideas, as long as he's alive, you'll never get your wife back.'

'I was just looking around,' Step growled sullenly. 'You say he's here?'

'What you need is a drink, boy,' Sonny said jovially. 'You deserve one. Give him a couple, Ethan, and I'll go scout around.'

He picked up his .44-40 repeating Winchester and disappeared toward the flagpole.

Upstairs, in Mike's office over the bank, Mike sat with a light blanket over his lap, the old Winchester across it, the Dutch binoculars to his eyes. He was leaning forward, almost against the big window pane, trying to peer through the darkness.

He picked up the Winchester by its stock and, with one hand, leaned over and poked the barrel against the blanket-rolled figure on the floor. 'Better get up, Hanse,' he whispered. 'That looks like Sonny heading down the street toward the livery. And I'd bet a hundred dollars it was Lon Perry I saw slipping into the livery corral a little while ago.'

Over in Kathy's kitchen, Ordway rose to his feet, his coffee cup empty. Doc Cartwright had leaned forward and wearily closed his eyes for a cat nap, his gray-goateed face, momentarily serene, cradled in his crossed arms. Koonce had gone back to his position on guard in the back door hallway.

Ordway tip-toed softly to the bedroom door and, feeling guilty of intruding, looked in. To his surprise Eric Randolph's eyes were open and unclouded. Vernell sat on one side of the bed and Mary Randolph on the other. Kathy had gone out on the front porch with coffee for her father.

'I hope I'm not intruding,' Ordway spoke gently.

'Come in, Channon,' Mrs. Randolph replied and rose to her feet. Her tired face was alight with a new happiness. 'It will take time but he's going to recover.'

Ordway stood with the big sombrero in his hand, the deadly pistol at his right hip. He looked down at the bandaged man.

'Seems to me, Eric, that it's about time you and I got on the same side of the fence, No, don't talk. Let me. I brought your herd back because I made you a promise. You've got roughly fourteen or fifteen hundred head of new spring calves and there'll be more of a drop that will increase the percentage. If we get this thing straightened out you and I can do some swapping of cattle to square things up. If we don't, it wouldn't have made any difference anyway.'

'Thank . . . you,' came weakly.

He went to the doorway and turned, tall and grim. Once again he looked like the terrible gunman, the killer they had known that first day. He didn't look at Vernell. He didn't dare, he felt that he had no right to after what she had witnessed. She stood looking at him, every fiber in her being, which he had said would be coarsened, crying out, but no sound came.

Ordway put on his sombrero. A faint grin broke the hard lines around his grim mouth. 'By the way, amigo,' he told the wounded man. 'As one man who has been shot in the back to another, that was a damned good piece of shooting you did on Harl Griddle. By the time you get back in the saddle, his kind will cut a wide trail around when they see you coming.'

Somewhere up in the front of the house a

door slammed. Hurried footsteps came running through the parlor. Kathy's skirts rustled as she came into the doorway beside Ordway.

She looked up at him, eyes wide with a new fear. Her face had lost its faint new color. 'Chann! It's Pa. He's gone!'

'Did you hear anything?' he rapped quickly.

'Nothing. His blanket is in the chair but his gun is gone.'

A little of the tension went out of Ordway. At least they hadn't taken him prisoner.

Ordway went into the kitchen and met Koonce. Koonce said calmly, 'Hanse always cussed that black mare of Step's about chewing herself loose, but I guess I forgot when I looped her reins. She's gone, Chann, with your gun on the saddle.'

So it had come. They knew. All element of surprise had been destroyed, and Lon Perry had slipped away.

'We'd better get moving,' the ex-lawman grunted savagely.

Ordway shook his head. 'No, you've got a wounded man here they want dead. You've got three women that anything can happen to.'

189

He was busy jerking off his spurs and then the short *chaparajas*, slipping his gun belt back into place. Doc Cartwright came awake and got to his feet. He yawned and stretched.

'I've got my old rifle and a belt of shells out in the back of the buggy. Been carrying it under my canvases for quite some time. Poor Pete. This is one the limping old son-of-a-gun would have loved. He never stopped cussing me because of the job I did on that bullet-shattered tibia.'

Ordway slid the heavy belt of useless .45-70 cartridges over his head and slipped noiselessly out into the night. The livery was the nearest cover and he made it, walking fast but quietly. There was a slim chance that Lon Perry might have stepped over to his house not far away, but he would have told Koonce.

'I'll bet a hundred dollars Step has been slipping him watered down liquor to get back on his side,' Channon muttered darkly.

A dozen horses were in the corral where Ordway had fired a night shot at Sonny that missed, and another at one of his men that hadn't missed. They were awake, switching tails, and one or two walked restlessly as though impatient for breakfast. Ordway slid in along the poles and came to the shed under which he had saddled the black mare. Familiar odors came to his olfactory senses; the old dung and the new, feed dust and hay and harness, ammoniac odor of horse, and one or two more, somehow familiar, but not identified.

He looked up dazedly and some kind of intelligence blew away the mists in his clouded brain. 'Go on,' he muttered thickly. 'Do what you oughta done long time ago. Shoot me.'

Ordway blew out the candle. The man tried to get up and fell with a hard crash. Ordway heard him try to roll over, try to get up on all fours. Then Lon Perry dropped flat on his face and passed into merciful oblivion.

From the other end of the shed Sonny, rifle in hand and walking like a cat, heard the mumbles and the crash and grinned knowingly. Old Ethan. He never missed a bet. And neither did he, Sonny. He'd gone Ethan one better.

Lon Perry had held out four lip-licking days after a friend, paid by Sonny, had slipped into his ear the information that there were a couple of quarts of Hanse's

191

best whiskey hidden in the desk of the livery office.

Ordway heard the footsteps and flattened himself against the wall. He opened the sagging, weatherbeaten door to the office and let it hang naturally, using it as cover. His heart skipped a beat as Sonny's cat-like boot steps approached.

'Hey, Lon,' Sonny whispered grinningly in the night. 'That you in there, old-timer?' He heard a wheezing groan from the floor and risked a match.

He blew out the match, grinning his sneering grin, his eyes yellow-flecked. And while he was light-blind, Channon Ordway smashed into him. A strangled cry went out of the outlaw sheriff. He dropped the rifle and clawed for his gun. He tried to yell, to scream a warning, but a hand was at his throat. It had been this way so many years ago when he and Channon had fought that day when Sonny had Kathy down in the weeds.

Ordway smashed a fist into his face. He was raising it again to shut off Sonny's throat-loosed cry when something like a giant catamount landed squarely upon his back. An odor he had smelled but hadn't defined came to his nostrils. Indian.

They were all over him now; choking him down, holding him, dragging him back. Four of them had Sonny in vice-like grips and were ramming a dirty buckskin gag into his mouth, while others held his hands and jerked off his boots. Sonny's eyes were terrified as he smelled the smell of Ute, the same smell of the young squaws—though he hadn't been too concerned *then*.

'You quiet now,' a voice said in Ordway's ear and a breath like the odor of warm entrails smote his nostrils.

They released him and he straightened. He stood in silence as four figures carried a gagged, bootless, twisting, writhing, terrified rapist and killer toward the flagpole in front of the little flat-topped courthouse. On the very spot where Sonny had shot a saddled horse to death they held him while the flag rope was tied around his ankles.

Dawn was breaking swiftly as they hoisted him.

One of the figures jerked the gag from Sonny's mouth above the long, tawny hair hanging straight down. They broke into a run toward hidden horses. The men with Ordway disappeared. He walked over, had

193

picked up Sonny's repeater, noting automatically that the ammunition in his belt would fit it. The pine tree flagpole was a sliver against the awakening sky.

He stood there as Sonny, the tendons in his heels and hands slashed, hung there head down—one agonized scream after another coming from his throat.

Old White Buffalo had spoken of a coyote that climbed a tree from which the limbs had been cut.

Sonny Shackleford hung there with old Tobe Whitehouse's badge on his shirt front, and kept on screaming.

## CHAPTER FOURTEEN

Tulac settlement came awake in the manner of a wary man feeling a hand on his shoulder and a whisper. It made no sound but lay alert and listening as the screams rose and fell and then diminished into whimpers. Lights went on but nobody investigated. A dozen heavily armed men had been in virtual control of the town for days, and they knew Ethan Ordway.

The sky turned gray.

194

Ordway stood with Sonny's repeater in his hands, stony-faced, and, in a measure, helpless. He heard the sound of running feet and turned and both Henry Cartwright and Koonce hurried swiftly into the front corral. They ran past the office where Lon Perry was trying to roll over and came up beside Ordway near the water trough. This was where Step Eaton had struck down Kathy.

'What in God's name?' Doc asked.

Ordway pointed with the rifle. Sonny was flailing his arm weakly and calling, 'Ethan. Ethan. Help me.'

'The Utes slipped in and got him. Believe me, boys, I knew nothing about it. I had him down in the dirt when they jumped both of us.'

'What now?' Koonce asked, still breathing hard from the run.

'Ask Doc. He's the authority on such things. They cut the tendons in his heels and hands. Old Ute trick against an enemy they particularly hated.'

'Nothing I can do,' Cartwright said. 'Nothing I would do if I could. Hippocrates has been dead since 377 B.C. and the hell with the oath I took. Well, well. Take a look.'

Ethan and Step and the members of Sonny's outfit had emerged from the north entrance to Hansen's saloon. They made no effort to go to the stricken man hanging head down from the pole. They stood grouped, silent. They saw Ordway and Koonce and Doc, armed, down there in the livery corral. Ethan saw the dim faces of Mike and Hanse up there back of the big upstairs window in the bank, and he knew again they must die. All of them, including Doc. Well, it could be done and quite easily.

'God-all-mighty, Ethan,' one of the toughs almost whimpered. 'We just can't let him hang there. Can't get to him either. What are we—'

'Ethan,' called Sonny's pleading voice a hundred yards away. 'Help me. They cut my heels and wrists. Come get me down! Call Doc!'

Ethan turned to Step, who was pale and on the verge of losing three small drinks. 'Chann's Sharps is on the black mare's saddle. Best gun in the country. I know because Tim gave it to him.' His voice turned harsh. 'Go get it.'

He stood there in the full dawn, thinking of Sonny, who should have been his son.

He saw a tough little tow-head who'd worshipped him long before, and after, his father was lynched. A good cow thief, brand expert, a leader of rough men. Fast with a gun, and guts enough never to hesitate. He knew the right way to handle women too, with no nonsense. The same way Ethan had handled them.

There was a world, a very secret world, in which Ethan lived alone and shared with nobody; a world of dreams and lost echoes. And in some of these phantasies he had liked to imagine that Sonny was his own boy and that Ellen Ordway was alive and loved him as she had loved Tim and that they all three lived together on Pronghorn Ranch.

But her repeatedly ravaged body was dust, and Pronghorn was in ashes, and Sonny hung head down from a pine flagpole in front of the courthouse, his tendons Ute-cut.

Step Eaton came up and handed him the stubby looking rifle. 'There's one in the chamber,' Step said chokingly. 'I looked.'

'Then use it,' Ethan ordered harshly.

Step swallowed hard and shook his head, the bile in his throat as bitingly soured as it had been that day down in the Randolph's living room when he faced the man he'd shot in the back.

'I didn't think you had backbone enough,' Ethan sneered and reached for the outstretched weapon.

He cocked it and looked at the dangling figure. Step turned and hurried into Hanse's saloon. Once inside he ran through to the old south porch and the black mare. He almost held both hands over his ears. To his surprise, the black mare didn't rear or dodge when he picked up the reins. He stood holding them, looking past the curve of the old fort's log buildings; looking past the south tip of the livery toward his home over there on the west edge of the settlement.

He waited for the heavy roar of the big rifle.

Ethan stepped to a wooden awning support. He lifted the short barrel and laid it against a four-by-four and clamped it hard with a bear-claw hand. 'Ethan,' came Sonny's agonized cry. 'Ethan, help me.'

'Steady, boy!' Ethan Ordway cried out, and centered the front sight. The shot smashed the stillness and went rolling away over the lip of the promontory into Squaw Valley. The sound rocketed into the bowl that was Pronghorn Basin. It echoed old memories of Pete and Tobe Whitehouse and old man Shackleford and all the dothers. Ghosts of old memories.

It was echoed again as one of the outlaws pulled his pistol and began firing at the three men over in the livery corral. Rifles began to speak back. A man let out a yell and grabbed his arm. From over at the bank came the crash of prized glass and the sharp reports of two old Winchesters. The wounded man died and so did another beside him. Led by Ethan, the others dived inside the protection of Hanse's hewed log walls.

Over at the flagpole the figure of Sonny Shackleford hung silent and motionless.

'Get under cover,' Ordway yelled and broke for the protection of the shed.

He dropped to one knee and began to drive a stream of .44-70s aslant through the back door of Hanse's saloon.

At the old south porch, Step Eaton heard the popping of rifles from what sounded like a half-dozen different points. Doc Cartwright, agile for his age and profession, had sprinted out of the livery corral and made a dash for the courthouse, while Hanse and Mike drove a stream of fast levered slugs through the north door and the back room window. Doc was now working his Winchester, angling shots in along the east wall.

The north end was sealed up but the old south end, where the horses were racked, was still open in case the toughs decided to make a break for it. Inside the saloon Ethan stood back of the bar and calmly poured himself a drink. The walls were thick and they had food and water and ammunition, not to mention a bit of whiskey as needed. In the excitement no one had missed Step.

'Hey, Ethan, we oughta be gettin' outa here,' called one of the crouched outlaws from across the room.

'Why?' Ethan downed the drink. It burned into the partly healed gum tissue, but it felt good going down.

'We ain't got a chance to get at that bank.'

Ethan corked the bottle and wiped his mouth. His face turned grimly sardonic. 'Why bother to take it out, Joe? We'd only have to put it all back in later.'

A man laughed nervously. So did another. Suddenly they were roaring with coarse laughter.

Outside Step heard the laughter and a

gradual dying down of the first ammunition-wasting fire. He stood there with the black mare's reins in hand and looked at the town where he had been born. All the common sense he possessed told him to get aboard her and keep going until she dropped dead under him. But there was a girl down there in a stone-fronted home. His wife. He'd treated her like an Indian treated a dog. He'd done worse. He'd taken her unborn child out of her body.

He could go to her and beg forgiveness. He could tell her that he'd scattered all the outlaws' horses to make certain they didn't escape. He'd get down on his knees and beg, promise anything, if she'd forgive and come back to him.

He went to the hitch rack and flung loose the reins of the horses. He was up in leather, fast, now, like in the old days, and a wild yell went out of him. The horses broke and scattered away at a run and Step Eaton wheeled the mare. He drove her at a run toward his and Kathy's home.

Ordway and Koonce were coming out of the livery corral, heading at a dogtrot to get into position and thus seal off the south end of the saloon. Hanse already had run down the back stairs of the bank and, great belly bounding, was coming flat-footedly in from the east with the same thought in mind.

Then a black mare flashed by the opening near the store and was gone in a thunder of hooves. Koonce threw up the shotgun, then lowered it with a shake of his head. 'See you later,' he said. 'Hold 'em till I get back.'

'Give me your gun first,' Ordway said. 'I hope you have better luck this time.'

The deputy broke into a run, shotgun in hand. He ran awkwardly as men do who wear high heel boots.

On the front porch of the neat home, Kathy stood with Vernell, shading her eyes against the first curved tip of the rising sun. The shooting had settled down to a sporadic rifle or pistol shot. A footstep sounded and an old woman of nearly seventy came into view around the corner from her own home. Tobe Whitehouse's widow carried a blanket under one arm. A thin dewlap of dried skin hung from beneath her chin, but her old shoulders were still sturdy, her steps firm.

'I'm going over to that flagpole and cut Sonny down,' she said determinedly. 'No matter what he done, he don't deserve this. He never had a ma he knew, never had a chance. If we hadn't taken Robert in when his pa got killed over in Nevada it mighta been him hangin' out there.'

She strode away and Vernell left Kathy and ran after her. 'Wait, Mrs. Whitehouse. I'm coming with you.'

They were fifty yards from the house when a black mare, belly low at a hard run, came flashing toward the house. Step shot by the two women and hauled her down with a cruel hand. Her haunches were almost on the ground when he stepped from Ordway's Mexican saddle.

'Step!' Kathy cried out. 'What're you doin' here?'

'Kathy—honey, I had to see you again,' he pleaded. 'Listen, honey I've got to go away for a while but I had to see you first. I was all wrong about everything.'

He moved toward her and she instinctively backed up a step. 'Don't you come no nearer,' she cried out. 'You killed my baby.'

'Honey,' he begged. 'I was drunk, I was crazy jealous. I never done all the things they said I did. I didn't burn the Rocking R. Chann did. I swear I didn't shoot old Tobe in the back. Ethan did it. I—'

He didn't see the figure of the black-browed man coming at a lung-bursting long trot, shotgun in hand. His eyes were upon Kathy, and for just a few seconds he almost believed himself.

'Honey—'

'You get outa heah!' Kathy screamed at him, and looked around as though for a weapon. She found none and fled inside and bolted the door. Step Eaton hammered on it with his fist.

'Please, baby-doll—'

With one hand he pushed back his hair and then put on his hat. He shook his head slowly. It was too soon, he told himself. She needed more time.

He turned and walked out toward the mare, and then he knew that there was no more time left for himself. His right hand jerked down to his hip. A shotgun roared. Something struck him a screaming blow in the belly and knocked him down. He tried to roll over, to get up, then relaxed and clasped both hands over his blown-out belly.

A shadow and then several more loomed over him. He thought he saw Kathy's face, he wasn't sure. 'Bob,' he whispered chokingly.

'What is it?'

'In the house. Loose fireplace rock. I . . . wrote everything down. Miz Whitehouse. Please don't hate me. I done to old Tobe what . . . Ethan made me do.'

He closed his eyes and his bloody fingers unclasped themselves from across his blown-out stomach and fell limply to the ground. Another horse came running and Koonce rose from his knees as Hanse, aboard a captured outlaw horse, came up at an awkward gallop.

'Bob,' he bellowed. 'Get on that black mare and let's go! Chann has just gone in on 'em with two guns. It's a braceout!'

They were gone in a clatter of hooves and Vernell remembered a man who had kissed her and saw him dead and went back to the porch with a suddenly tired old woman beside her. Kathy Eaton picked up the blanket her father had used to keep away the chill while he sat guard during the chilly nights. She went out and spread it over the body of Step, leaving only the once handsome face in view. Miniature balls of water ran down from both her large, dark-circled eyes.

'Did you love him, Kathy?' Vernell felt herself compelled to ask.

'I hated him,' Kathy said tonelessly. 'He

beat me when he was drunk and he killed my baby. He was just plain no good. But he was my lawful husband.'

She covered the dead man's face and tucked the blanket in under his shoulders. 'I better go see if your pa might need somethin'.'

There was a certain strength and dignity as she walked toward the porch where Mary Randolph also stood shading her eyes with a hand.

## CHAPTER FIFTEEN

When the bearded, louse-ridden old buckskin men had first wintered in the lee of the promontory's rim back in the 1830's, it had been an ideal place to loaf in brush and skin shelters, swap lies and scratch, and watch for Utes in the valley and the basin below.

When the tide of law began to push lawless men farther west, and the first hunted men showed up in the camp, the snarling old trappers moved on. The outlaws remained.

Hanse had been one of the first to

arrive. He had built his cabin for a big man and built it high enough so that a man six and one half feet wouldn't bump his head when he straightened. He set up his plank bar between two tree stumps and told new arrivals such as Tobe Whitehouse and Shackleford and, later, Ethan and Tim Ordway that whiskey was cash; that he was tired of running; that come law-hell and high water and the Utes here he damn well stayed.

They elected Tobe 'sheriff' that winter, and within a year Hanse had a dozen wanted men busy cutting trees and building for the future. He had built his sprawling place, leaving a door to his cabin in the west wall near the end of the bar, and in the cabin Hanse had slept and batched and served his customers at any time of the day and night for more than thirty years, going on forty.

This door was now locked from the inside—Ethan having found that out at once after Hanse's six-shooter covered himself out of the place.

Channon Ordway slipped in between two of the old buildings. He opened a door, still hung with rawhide hinges, and slipped inside Hanse's sanctum where the weekly poker games were held.

It was strange, but he had never been in this old cabin in his life. He nor any other kid in town. After the shack became a lean-to, it became a sanctum for a few men of the old days and no others. Ordway looked at the wall bunks, the stove and table, and two twelve-inch planks nailed between two pine stumps.

He moved to the door, his spurless heels making no sound on the hard earth. He could hear muffled voices beyond the rawhide hinges. There was a heavy bar locked into cleats. With Koonce's six-shooter in his belt, Ordway carefully lifted the hand hewed four-by-six. After forty years of nightly use it was as smooth as new paint.

A rifle shot crashed out inside the building and then another. A muffled voice yelled gleefully: 'I knocked out the rest of Mike's fancy window. Next time he shows his head I've got him!'

And that was why Ordway had to go out. There was a thing that had to be done and done quickly, a calculated risk of himself lest some more people outside die. And there was a compelling fire of hatred and vengeance to be wreaked upon a man